TALES OF THE

UNIDENTIFIED

MAN

JIM MORRIS

&

DAN SULLIVAN

Dedicated to the late, great, Jim Morris whose untimely passing left more for you and me.

We'd all be happier with less if we could have him back.

Tales of The Unidentified Man

Published on a barstool in the U.S.A by:

OLD STONE PUBLISHING

Old Stone Publishing
Boise, ID 83714
info@oldstonepublishing.com
First Edition
ISBN: 9781693356612

Printed in the United States of America

Foreword

The summer after Jim passed, I received a call from our friend and author, Dan Sullivan. He said, "Sharon, I've finished writing the book that Jim and I had been discussing." I was a little skeptical, but after the first few pages, I was hooked. After suggesting a different ending, we published *Tales from the Land of No Mondays* in October of 2017.

After the success of *No Mondays*, I challenged Dan to write a book based on one of my favorite songs, *Tarpon Jim*. Dan said, "You want me to write a novel based on a three-hundred-word song?" I did, and a year later we released *The Tales of Tarpon Jim* which became very popular among Jim's fans.

Last fall, Dan and I were kicking around ideas for a third book. I suggested Jim's song, *Unidentified Man* and after months of work, it became a reality. Jim used to say, "How do I get a finger like that?" My 'directing finger' seems to work pretty well too!

Thank you, Dan, for turning Jim's music into wonderful novels, for "filling in the gaps" in Jim's songs. Thanks to Beth, his amazing editor, Kim over at Deranged Doctor for the cover design, Dave Monahan for his input, and to Amy Sullivan for her support on this journey, and for supporting us on journeys yet to be taken.

And thanks to all of you, Jim's amazing friends and fans for the outpouring of love and support over the years.

Sharon Morris
Punta Gorda, Florida
September 2019

Key Largo

Islamorada

Duck Key

Big Pine Key Marathon

Key West

The
Bahamas

Pelican Lake ———— West Side
National Park

Varadero

La Teja

Matanzas

Isabela de Sagua

Cardenas

CUBA

Sagua La

I wrote this song one evening during a violent summer thunderstorm. I was on the beach on Little Gasparilla Island in southwest Florida. I have always been intrigued by the sense of romance and adventure in the exploits of the pilots who fly contraband. This song is about the quiet desperation of living on the fringe.

Jim Morris

CHAPTER ONE

They were going to crash. It wasn't a matter of if or when; it was only a matter of where. His engine was failing. Oil sprayed onto his windshield as a thick, putrid smoke filled the cockpit. Daylight was visible through the newly punctured holes in his right wing. The little Continental six-piston engine was still running but sounded like it was about to come apart. Tweaking the fuel-air mixture, he tried to coax a bit more power out of her, but his plane was dying a quick death.

The 37mm tracer rounds that had hit them had come out of nowhere. They had riddled the plane, shooting away much of the engine cowling and filling the right wing and fuselage with bullet holes. He heard his spotter in the back seat of the tiny O-1 Birddog scream when they got hit, but he hadn't heard a sound from him since. When he glanced over his shoulder at the man slumped in the back, it didn't look good.

Blood ran down his own leg. He would have felt a hot, stabbing pain if not for the adrenaline coursing through his body and his single focus on getting the aircraft back to friendly territory.

The only reachable clearing he could see was to the northwest of them, but the good guys were to the south. The ground below and anything to the north were controlled by Vietnamese regulars. He struggled to keep the little plane in the air as he gently entered a banking righthand turn. Extending the flaps in hopes of decreasing his glide slope, he watched in horror as the inboard pivot point failed on the right flap, causing it to come loose. Unfortunately, the outboard hinge held, and the loose piece of flap hanging off his wing increased the drag, slowing the plane even further.

In forty-seven flights, he had never taken as much as a single bullet hole. Now all he could do was watch as his plane came apart around him.

"Mayday, mayday, mayday! Helix Five-One, we are hit and going down!" He glanced down at the chart strapped to his knee so he could report a position, when he realized he was going to hit the tree tops. All he could do was hang on.

***

He had been attracted to her from the first moment he saw her. She was a beautiful girl. It was her eyes that attracted most boys' attention. Set just a tad further apart than most, they were almost too large for her face. Dark, deep, and intense, they had always been her most striking feature. When she was younger, people would stop her parents in public just to comment on her beautiful eyes.

He had first noticed Alice in school. She was quiet, shy, and mysterious. She kept mostly to herself and seemed to have only a few friends. She never attended the school's football or basketball games, and she was never seen at dances or anywhere outside of the regular class schedule. Alice seemingly appeared at 8:00am and disappeared at 3:00pm.

She dismissed his attempts to speak to her and ignored his juvenile advances. It was pure luck that he was assigned to her lab group in biology class, forcing her acknowledge him. He played it cool, showing no signs that he liked her. He was polite, kind, and helpful, and that was what she first noticed about him.

His first success in their relationship came when he told her he only lived a few blocks from her. If they walked home together, they could discuss the project. He gave no indication of anything else, keeping the discussion focused on the assignment. When they arrived in front of her house, he said goodbye before walking around the corner, then around the block. He walked back to the school and six blocks in the opposite direction to get home.

He walked her home almost every day for weeks. Their talks were gradually less about biology and more about each other. One day on the sidewalk in front of her home, she said, "You know what I can't figure out?" He shrugged his shoulders. "I can't figure out why you walk me home every day, ten blocks out of your way, and you've never once tried to kiss me."

The smell of her perfume and the taste of her kisses were fresh in his mind when Orv woke. The searing pain from his leg wound and the throbbing of his jaw overpowered the pleasant dream, bringing him back to the smoking carcass of an airplane lying on the humid, stinking hillside of the Asian jungle. His seat had broken free in the crash, and his face had slammed into the instrument panel. With his good leg, he pushed back, giving him room to crawl out of the twisted wreckage. Orv fell onto the ground and lay panting in pain for several minutes, wondering how long he had been unconscious.

As his brain started to awaken, he looked around and put together where he was and what had happened. "Ricky," he said out loud as he remembered his spotter. He crawled to the plane and pulled open what was left of the door, Ricky was covered with blood but still breathing. He knew there was nothing he could do to help him. Moving him might worsen his injuries. The little first aid kit they carried wasn't going to have what he needed to stem Ricky's bleeding.

When he heard voices down the hill below them, his training started to kick in. He reached next to Ricky and pulled out his M-16 then retrieved his own carbine that was strapped next to his seat. He checked the .45 pistol he carried on his side to make sure it was loaded. With the weapons ready, he crawled to the uphill side of the aircraft and got ready for a fight.

Orv thought he saw movement in the jungle below him, but the voices had gone silent. They had likely spotted the wreckage. He peered into the foliage on the other side of the aircraft so intently that he never saw the five men creeping up behind him. He never had a chance to put up a fight. He didn't fire a single round.

They were on him in seconds, pinning him to the ground while they tied his hands behind his back. Setting him up against a tree, they searched the plane for anything useful. Two soldiers pulled Ricky from the wreckage and threw him onto the ground. He was pale, ashen, and he didn't seem to be breathing any longer.

Ten feet away, a man who appeared to be the leader squatted and stared at Orv. He appeared to be assessing the American, sizing him up. His eyes were yellowed from previous bouts of malaria. His face was hollow and mean, showing his hatred of the big, well-dressed enemy he opposed. Finally, he stood and said something to the others. They responded by dragging Orv to his feet. The leader pointed downhill, and they poked an AK-47 barrel into his back, making it clear they were leaving. He looked over at Ricky and said out loud, "Sorry, buddy."

The yellow-eyed leader mimicked him. "Sowee butee." He laughed then spit towards the body on the ground.

Searing pain in his leg caused him to limp badly. He struggled with each step. They pushed him forward, continually prodding him with the weapon, jabbing it over and over into his back.

They had only walked fifty meters when the helicopters passed low overhead going north. He heard a Cobra fly over followed by two HH-53 Jolly Green Giants. He didn't need to look up; he knew what they were and what they contained. The Bell Cobra attack helicopter was likely escorting the Jolly Green Giants out of the airbase at Tan Son Nhut. Each contained well-trained and highly motivated members of the 3rd Aerospace Rescue and Recovery Group whose sole job was to recover downed pilots.

Yellow Eyes knew what the chopper represented too. They would land their troops in the clearing to the north and start sweeping south. He knew if he didn't move quickly, his tiny squad would be caught between the pissed-off Americans and the ridge behind him. They didn't have time to build a stretcher, and they couldn't make the injured pilot move any faster.

He ordered his squad to stop and conferred with two of the other men while Orv leaned against a tree, trying to take the weight off his throbbing right leg. Once the thirty-second conference was completed, the commander shouted orders to his men, who immediately started moving off in a different direction, heading west rather than north. As his men disappeared into the jungle, Yellow Eyes stepped back towards the much larger American. He shouted something at him, a statement full of vile hatred. Then he raised his AK-47 and shot Orv in the chest.

***

In a sweet dream, a wide stretch of beach extended before them as far as they could see. Gentle waves lapped up on the beach, playfully splashing their feet as they walked hand in hand. The beach was framed by a long string of palm trees lining the edge of the sand. Frangipani bushes and hibiscus shrubs flowered under the palms, each donating their own particular scent to an incredible day. As they walked along the water, a pod of dolphins appeared just beyond the surf, playfully rolling while the sun reflected off their wet skins. They looked like benevolent ghosts on the shimmering water.

Alice had never looked so beautiful. She wore a sheer white coverup over her swimsuit, her hair was pulled back, and she had tucked a flower behind her ear. Her smile gave away the love she felt for him. Orv had never been so happy. They talked about their future, about children, and about growing old together. They promised each other that in the difficult times, when the conflicts that inevitably happen between two people created stress in their marriage, they would come here to the beach and walk hand in hand while they worked it out. The beach and the ocean had a calming influence and a healing effect. The ocean would never fail them; therefore, they would never fail.

***

Orv woke from the dream to a confusing and chaotic scene. An Air Force medic leaned over him, yelling at him to breathe. He struggled to take a breath, but every ounce of air he took in increased the stabbing pain in his chest. To his left, men crouched and fired their weapons out into the jungle. Something exploded just beyond his feet, throwing the young, wide-eyed medic onto him. The corpsman's face was very close to his. He made a series of animal-like grunting sounds while his eyes searched wildly for something. Blood appeared from his nose and mouth, then he rolled off to the side and coughed twice before he died.

The only thing Orv could do to help the medic was to do the last thing he had asked, to breathe. He helplessly watched the firefight that was taking place without him. He saw other soldiers get hit, some writhing in pain, others simply falling over, and he tried to breathe. Above him, he could see a thin patch of blue sky through the jungle's canopy. As he felt himself starting to slip away, he saw another O-1 Birddog, a tiny unarmed two-seater Cessna fly past. It comforted him to know that they weren't alone. He forced himself to breathe, to stay conscious, and to keep breathing.

***

Lightning cracked in the western sky. The storm was fast approaching. The surf churned white with rollers, crashing on the shore. A noise above the rumble caught their attention as a seaplane swooped in just over the tops of the palms and sat down in the turbulent waters and swirling winds.

Looking over at the newbie sitting next to him at the wheel, Ken Hopkins said, "Let's get this over with before that storm hits."

Jack advanced the throttles, bringing the old Springer 32 up on plane as he turned to chase down the de Havilland Beaver that had just landed in the strait off Snipe Keys. The old high-winged plane on floats looked like it had been in the islands its entire life. The once shiny orange and white paint was now dull and faded and dirty. Exhaust and oil stains ran down both sides of the fuselage. Painted on the side was the logo of a long out-of-business fishing guide, *Tarpon Jim Fishing Charters*. The plane was a perfect match for the old sport fishing boat that chased it, the stolen *Lucky Strike III*. The boat, sporting its own sunbaked and oxidized paint, had survived thirty-four years of neglect to live an infamous second career.

It was a simple job: pick up a couple of hundred pounds of prime Columbian from the plane and deliver it to a beach on No Name Key. The two guys on the boat would split about five thousand dollars for three hours of work and the tourists and residents of the Lower Keys would be happy and high for another week or so.

Hopkins took the captain's chair as they closed on the plane. He told Jack to drop a couple of bumpers over the stern; they would back into the plane's float behind the port side wing. As they backed towards the aircraft, the door near the rear of the plane opened, and a man dressed in a baseball cap, tan khakis, and a horribly wrinkled Hawaiian shirt stepped down onto the float.

The pilot, with his unkempt beard, disheveled clothes, and slack posture defied all of Jack's pre-conceived notions of how a pilot should look. He was familiar with the stark white uniforms, the pressed shirts and dark slacks of the pilots he had encountered on commercial flights. This guy looked like an old drunk straight out of a seedy bar.

Without a word, the pilot started pulling sacks from the cargo door of the old plane and handed them across to Jack while Ken kept the Springer snugged up to the plane with just a bit of back throttle. He handed across fourteen bags, gave a quick nod, then waved up to Ken on the flying bridge. With that, he climbed back into the plane and pulled the door shut behind him. Not a single word between them had been spoken.

The Beaver's engine caught then coughed and belched a cloud of blue smoke before it throttled up. Jack watched the plane turn and plow into the short swells, towards the approaching storm to the west as they headed east towards their drop location. The plane accelerated then hopped once, coming off the water about two feet before settling back down and then springing skyward and turning south.

Skimming just above the tree line, Orv flew the sixty-year-old plane south until he crossed Highway 1 near Bahia Honda State Park, then he turned east, flipped on his transponder, and began to climb. At two thousand feet, he radioed Miami Center asking for vectors to the Miami Seaplane Base. He was just another pilot on another routine flight from the Keys to Miami.

He eyed the approaching storm that still threatened from the west then glanced at his fuel. The seven-hundred-mile trip from Miami to the Bahamas, to the Keys, and back to Miami stretched his fuel range if he didn't hit weather. If he could get around the northern edge of the front, he would easily make it home with plenty of reserve fuel. If he got caught in the buffeting winds and pounding rain, it could be a much different story. Fifteen minutes later, Miami gave him a direct course to the northeast, and he breathed a sigh of relief. He would clear the storm without any problem.

It was another successful run. Another twenty-five thousand dollars would appear in his bank account. Every trip used to be a big adventure, but at this point, it was just a job and nothing more.

***

Alice had taken back her maiden name after the divorce. The years after her marriage crumbled had fostered a number of changes: a new address, a new name, and a new and somewhat frightening sense of independence. It had nurtured several positive changes. She lost the ten pounds she had been battling with for years, she found a renewed interest in her hobby of photography, and her career seemed to blossom.

From an early age, Alice Weingarten's dream had been to become an attorney and eventually a judge, but those dreams just hadn't panned out. She had gone to college, obtaining a degree in Criminal Justice with a focus on pre-law. She was accepted into law school, but on her husband's small salary as a cargo pilot, they simply couldn't afford it. She went to work for the Dade County Sheriff's Department to save up enough money for law school, but after several years of uniform patrol, she was promoted to detective and then transferred into Narcotics. She liked her job, so her dreams faded.

A few months after her divorce was final, a phone call changed her life. As the interagency liaison to the Sheriff's Department, she worked closely with the various agencies in the area, including the DEA. Her work hadn't gone unnoticed. She was offered a position as a Special Agent for the Drug Enforcement Agency out of the Miami Divisional Office. It was a huge leap forward, and she vowed to make those superiors who took the chance on her proud.

Working for the DEA out of Southern Florida was a dream job. There was no lack of work; drugs poured over the beaches and into the harbors from hundreds of points south of the U.S. The Agency was well funded, the pay was good, and the assignments were exciting. Before she realized it, she had become an adrenaline junkie. She liked the high a bust gave her. She liked the feeling of taking down a dealer, she loved dismantling a drug ring. Entering a warehouse full of drugs and gun-toting bad guys was almost an erotic high. She liked it and wanted more.

***

The approach to the Miami Seaplane Base took him just east of Key Biscayne. He passed Virginia Key to his left and then turned west at Fisher Island. He followed Government Cut down the main channel between a line of shiny white cruise ships docked at Dodge Island and the MacArthur Causeway. Orv set the Beaver down gently just a few hundred yards short of the base. He had perfected his landing here, leaving him with a very short distance to taxi.

After being towed up the ramp by the base's rusty old tug, he secured the plane and drove his beat-up Toyota Camry towards his little apartment in Westchester. He stopped along the way to pick up a case of beer and some Chinese take-out at a little place he liked off Coral Way. In his apartment, he cracked open a beer to accompany his white-boxed dinner, then settled in his old recliner to mindlessly surf channels and drink beer until he either fell asleep or passed out.

It wasn't the existence he had imagined when he was a younger man. If he ever took stock of his life, he would probably realize how truly pathetic it had become. He was alone, he had no real friends, his income came from a risky source with a dubious future. His only possessions were his old airplane and a small offshore bank account. He got up from the chair and grabbed a second beer from the fridge, then settled back to watch a movie he had seen at least a dozen times.

***

Alice wasn't afraid to admit it: she was both nervous and excited to be called to a big meeting at the National Headquarters of the Drug Enforcement Agency in Washington D.C. After the request to join the day-long meeting, the D.C. office had booked her flight and reserved her a room at the Renaissance, which was adjacent to the headquarters building on K Street. She checked in, then was taken out by her local counterparts to the Old Ebbitt Grill for a wonderful dinner. She enjoyed a restful night's sleep, woke early, worked out, then got ready for her big day.

She wasn't disappointed; she was greeted by Cindy Muir, the DEA Administrator's Chief of Staff. She was hustled in for a quick meet and greet with Paul Campbell, the acting administrator, then hurried to a conference room where she was introduced to a table full of people whose names she would have a hard time remembering. She gave a two-minute off-the-cuff talk about herself, and then as if on cue, the moment she finished, Paul Campbell entered the room and took the chair at the head of the table.

"Thank you all for coming," he said. "If you haven't figured it out yet, you're all here by design. You have each been identified as a valuable resource in your divisional office and a potential key player in a new operation we are launching on all fronts. We've had significant successes in stopping the large shipments of drugs that flow across our borders. With improved intelligence and increased cooperation from our foreign counterparts, we have made a huge dent in the massive shipments coming into U.S. ports. But billions of dollars of drugs still come into our country through smaller distribution channels, the little guys, the fishing boats, private cars, and small airplanes. Our next initiative is to assist local law enforcement, Andy and Barney out on the street, U.S. Border Patrol, Homeland Security, and the Coast Guard in stopping those smaller shipments. That's why you're here. Let's get started."

Alice listened intently as she took notes and asked many questions. The focus of the DEA in Florida had always been on the large-quantity busts, leaving the small shipments to local law enforcement. But the DEA had gotten so good at finding the big cargos that the cartels had nearly stopped sending them. They now sent their drugs on an armada of small boats and a fleet of little planes. Campbell made it clear the people in the room were responsible for figuring out how to stop an invasion of minnows and mosquitos, a nearly impossible task.

During a break, Alice sipped on a cup of coffee and thought of the local police in the town where she grew up. They were good people. Some were fathers to her friends— they coached baseball and football and they were ordinary people. They were outgunned by the cartels—the druggies had better boats and planes, and in some cases, better intelligence than the locals.

Growing up in the little Southern Florida town of Cape Coral, Alice Weingarten always felt lucky that she had a nearly perfect childhood. Her father was a social worker, her mother a housewife. She had two sisters with whom she had gotten along most of the time. Their little family ate dinner together almost every night and attended church every Sunday morning. She worked hard to get good grades and played clarinet in the high school band. During her junior year, she met Orville Hendricks, a quiet but polite boy in her class who was bonkers for her. They dated, and eventually, she fell in love with him and his dreams.

After high school, they both went to college at Southern Florida State. Alice chased her dream of becoming a lawyer, Orv wanted to be a pilot. She imagined an idyllic life as a lawyer, then a judge, married to a dashing pilot who wore a white uniform with epaulets on his shoulders. Orv turned her dreams on edge when he announced after his sophomore year that he had signed up with the U.S. Army and was heading to Fort Rucker, Alabama to learn to fly.

At first, she was angry with him for not discussing it with her, but he was so excited that his permanent grin didn't fade, even as she yelled at him. The Vietnam war had been dragging on for years, but the recruiter had told him that the real need for pilots was elsewhere. The war was consuming all the experienced pilots. He was promised the need for newer aviators was in either the United States or Europe.

There would always be those moments in life that she would never forget. She remembered the evening when he surprised her at college, looking so dapper in his dress uniform. He found her playing frisbee with friends, and there in front of all of them knelt and asked her to marry him. She was dumbfounded, she didn't know what to say, then he told her he was being deployed to Vietnam. She said yes, and they kissed. Four days before he was deployed, they were married at sunset on the beach at Anna Maria Island.

Eleven months later, another moment came that she would never forget. She received a phone call telling her that he had been wounded. For more than a week, she tried to find out where he was and how badly he was hurt, but the flow of information was a trickle at best. Finally, she learned he was in Japan. She was trying to make preparations to go to Japan when she learned he had been flown to Letterman General Hospital in San Francisco. Two days later, she stood before a young officer at the front desk at Letterman who told her he might be there, but it would not be possible to see him.

Alice had never been one to back down from a fight. She tossed out Senator Gurney's name, she quoted legal cases with precedence that had nothing to do with a wife's ability to see her injured husband. She made such a stink that the poor officer decided to let her in just to get her away from his desk.

As she stood next to Orv's bed, she realized why they didn't want her to see him. At first, she wasn't even certain it was her husband. His head was wrapped, his jaw wired shut. He had a massive dressing covering his chest and a cast on his right leg. Tubes drained fluids into bags below his bed. His eyes would open at the sound of her voice, but he didn't seem to see her. He would stare blindly towards the ceiling then close his eyes again until she squeezed his hand or spoke to him.

Doctors and nurses at the understaffed hospital rushed here and there. Nobody seemed to be able to provide much in the way of answers. It seemed like the hospital was nothing more than a warehouse of wounded soldiers. They received enough care to survive; recovery was up to them.

Finally, after determining that she wasn't going to go away, a kind nurse on break asked Alice to walk with her. She followed her out onto the hospital grounds, where they walked across the Presidio and talked. Nurse Gonzales explained that Orv's injuries were likely life-changing. His jaw and his leg would heal, but he had lost so much blood from his chest wound that they weren't sure how badly his brain and other organs might have been affected. Only time would tell.

Alice loved Orv with all of her heart. Time was all she had.

Over the next several days, he seemed to awaken, a little at a time. His eyes looked at her and seemed to focus on her face. When she asked him to blink if he could understand her, he blinked, and then a tear appeared. A day later, he managed a thin smile. When she squeezed his hand, he squeezed back. She sat next to him every day for a week, reading to him.

One day, as she read Hemmingway's *Island in the Sky* to him, a soldier with bandaged eyes two beds over asked if she would speak just a little louder. "With all due respect to your man there," said the blind man, "you have the most beautiful voice I have ever heard." Alice asked that the man be moved next to Orv when that bed became vacant.

After ten days, Orv could manage a few words. After two weeks, he started to hold things with his hands and to move his legs. Doctors told her that his recovery would never be a hundred percent, but with time and hard work, he might be able to walk again someday. They told her his speech would always be labored. He would never live a normal life.

When Alice became frustrated and scared by what the doctors were doing and the methods they were suggesting, Nurse Adela Gonzales again took her by the hand and walked out of the hospital. In a lightly falling rain, she stopped, looked Alice in the eyes, and then said, "Those doctors don't know squat. They make their best guesses based on what they have seen in the past. They don't know your man, and they don't know you. If you want something, it's up to you to make it happen."

Wiping her tears, Alice said, "I'm not a doctor. I don't know the best course of treatment. What they are doing and suggesting doesn't make sense, does it?"

Adela cringed. "I'm a soldier. I can't second guess my superior officers. But you need to understand something. Doctors and nurses are nothing more than technicians and advisors. The decisions are in your hands, the results are in God's."

With that, Alice smiled, wiped away her tears, and marched back into the hospital. From that minute forward, she directed Orv's care, based on his doctor's suggestions. It was clear that she was in charge. As soon as she could, she got him transferred to Fort Rucker Army Hospital in Alabama. Fort Rucker was two thousand miles closer to home and she hoped staffed with sensible people from the south rather than the knuckleheads from California.

CHAPTER TWO

Over the years, Orv had taught himself to drink defensively. He found that if he drank enough, he would eventually either pass out or fall into a heavy sleep. He seemed to dream less in an alcohol-induced slumber. The nights when he didn't successfully drink himself to unconsciousness, he would lie awake thinking about her. When exhaustion took over and sleep finally came, he was often visited by Yellow Eyes. He was haunted by the angry little man with the beady eyes and dirty face who repeatedly fired a weapon into his chest then spit on him while laughing and saying, "Sowee butee."

His two sinister ghosts refused him peace, one he hated and feared, the other he loved, almost more than life itself. After a night haunted by his ghosts, he would spend too much time dwelling on them and on his past. While flying, he sometimes wondered if nosing his plane into the ocean at three hundred knots would end his horrors and heartache forever. At times, it seemed that dying would be easier than living. He continued to live because he was too stubborn to give in to either of his demons.

He was awakened by the ringing of his cell phone. He searched for his phone while recognizing the symptoms of a raging hangover. "Hello," he said while making the mistake of looking out the window at the bright sunlight.

"The boss wants to see you this afternoon, four o'clock at the Parrot," said the familiar voice on the other end of the line.

Orv laid his head back on his pillow and coughed. "Tell the boss to screw himself."

"Four o'clock at the Parrot," the voice said before the line went dead.

It took him a moment to focus on the time display on his phone. It was a little after ten in the morning. He cursed and hit the bed with the back of his fist. The last thing he wanted to do today was spend four hours driving to Key West for a ten-minute meeting.

Sitting up on the edge of the bed, he took five aspirin from the bottle he kept on his night stand then washed them down with a big gulp of Pepto-Bismol. He stumbled to the kitchen, where he found a cold beer in the fridge and downed it in four swallows. Leaning against the counter, he decided he wasn't going to do battle with the crazy flocks of tourists and their motorhomes on Highway 1 today. He picked up his phone and poked at the screen.

"Seaplane Base," came the answer.

"Scotty, it's Orv. Can you put four hundred pounds of fuel on my plane? I'll be over in about an hour."

"Hey, Orv. Yes, we'll put four hundred pounds on seventy-one whiskey tango and have her pulled around to the ramp before eleven," he confirmed, obviously talking with one of his employees in the room at the same time.

"Thanks," he replied before he ended the call. He grabbed a second beer and headed for the shower.

***

Her meetings ended just in time for her to catch a cab to Reagan National for her flight home. As Alice slowly made her way down the plane's aisle, held up by people trying to shoehorn ridiculously sized bags in the overhead compartments, she noticed a man sitting by the window in the exit row. He wore a soiled cap and sported a week-old growth of beard. He didn't look much like her ex-husband, but he certainly reminded her of him.

Alice hadn't seen her ex in seven or eight years; in fact, it might have been as many as ten years. She wondered what he was up to, how he was getting along. Over the years, the pain associated with everything they had gone through had faded. She had always told her friends and family that she loved him, there was simply too much wreckage, too much debris between them.

As she settled in her seat, she found herself thinking back to the years they had spent together. They had so many good years before bad decisions and bad luck started to grind away at them. He used to tell her that life was a rollercoaster. When things were at their worst, when they were at the bottom, it was time to get excited because they were about to head back up towards the top. But for so many years, they just seemed to bounce along the bottom. Finally, the stress of it all simply tore them apart. It was probably nobody's fault.

As the plane accelerated down the runway, she realized that she'd like to see him again someday. It would be fun to catch up, to find out what he was doing. There were things she wanted to say to him. She wanted him to know that she didn't blame him at all for what they had gone through; it wasn't all his fault. When she thought about it for a few minutes, none of it was his fault. They were just victims of life's circumstances. She missed her friend.

***

Scotty helped him roll the plane down the ramp and into the water. Orv leapt onto the float as the plane reached the water's edge, his flipflop-covered feet barely getting splashed. As the aircraft drifted out into the bay, he climbed into the cockpit, flipped the master power switch, then pumped the wobbler pump below the instrument panel a half a dozen times to prime the engine. He turned on the ignition and hit the starter. After a couple of spins, the engine coughed, belched a cloud of blue smoke, then caught and roared to life. He pointed the plane downwind, taxiing at low idle towards the line of cruise ships, then buckled in and pulled on his headset.

After checking the fuel level, the oil pressure, and the oil temp, he radioed Miami Air Traffic Control and stated his intentions. By the time he had taxied far enough downwind to turn and safely take off into the wind, his oil temperature had risen to one forty and Miami ATC had given him a complicated routing south to Homestead. Some days, getting out of Miami's busy airspace was the biggest challenge of the flight.

Turning a hundred and eighty degrees to the northwest, he advanced the throttle and propeller then listened for any telltale sounds of trouble as the big radial engine roared. With eighty-five knots showing on the airspeed indicator, he pulled back on the yoke as a gust hit the nose of the plane, lifting it out of the water. He climbed to two thousand feet and turned south, carefully following the directions he had written on the pad strapped to his thigh.

Southwest of Homestead, he flew over a waypoint out in the middle of the Everglades known as "Ranger Station," the Everglades Visitors Center. A minute later, he flew over the Florida National Parks administrative and maintenance buildings. From there, he would be in the middle of nowhere for the next forty-five miles. The Everglades and south into the Keys were some of the most inhospitable, unforgiving, and beautiful land he had ever had the privilege of flying over.

It was a beautiful day. Clouds gathered to the east, out over the Atlantic, but they didn't look threatening. It was a warm day, but the air was relatively smooth. The winds were calm over the Glades and the turbulence was nearly non-existent, rare for this time of year. He could have brought a cup of coffee with him and successfully drank it without most of it ending up on him. Flying on days like this, doing nothing illegal, with no time constraints, reminded him of why he loved to fly.

Ahead and below him, and almost a hundred and eighty degrees out his port and starboard windows, he could see the edge of the Everglades and the waters of Florida Bay. The bay is a thousand-square miles area at the southern tip of mainland Florida that consists of interconnected basins and mangrove islands. The area, extending from Florida City to Matecumbe and back up to Marco Island, with a thin strip descending beyond Key West, provided some of the most remarkable habitat for wildlife in the world. The bay also provided him with thousands of remote stretches of protected water to land and offload his illegal goods.

On a day like this, he didn't need his instruments or GPS to find his destination. He followed the line of islands off his left side and the blue line of deeper water out his right. Where they intersected was Matecumbe. From there, he would turn southwest and with the string of islands off the left side of the plane, following them to Key West.

His stomach growled, reminding him that he hadn't eaten breakfast. He checked his watch and decided that a cracked conch sandwich at the Lorelei sounded pretty good. He set his radio to 122.85 and started a lazy bank to the left to line up with the southern tip of Islamorada.

Pressing the comm button on the top of his yoke, he said, "Islamorada traffic, Beaver seventy-one whiskey tango is five miles northwest of the Lorelei, inbound water landing at Barley Basin." The winds looked calm, but he noticed the slightest swell rolling on the bay to the east. The safest approach happened to be the quickest too, straight in. "Islamorada traffic, Beaver seventy-one whiskey tango, final into the Lorelei, southeast water landing."

Orv set the flaps for landing and cut the throttle back, almost to idle. Gliding above the water, he looked for boats, logs, fish traps, or any number of other obstacles that might ruin his day. Seeing only clear water, he leveled the plane about ten feet above the bay and let his speed bleed off as he watched the swells. The plane had just enough speed to carry it over the crest of a swell, then he flared, stalling the aircraft by pulling the nose up a few degrees as the pontoons touched the water between swells. She settled in the bay, and in a matter of seconds, transitioned from being an airplane to a boat.

After landing in the channel just off the island, he taxied around the east end of the mangroves. He was happy to see a brightly painted blue, yellow, and white Cessna 206 seaplane wearing the logo of Miami Seaplanes backed into the beach. Thirty feet off the beach, he cut the engine, unbuckled, shut off the master switch, and opened the door. As he climbed down the strut steps to the float, he turned and reached behind his seat and grabbed a small anchor attached to a rope. His feet hit the float just as the plane mushed into the sandy beach. He closed the door and was excited to see Kevin Karcher, his friend and the pilot of the 206 on the beach to help him.

"Kevin, you old bastard. How are you?" Orv shouted as he tossed the anchor onto the beach.

"Living the dream," he replied.

Kevin dug the anchor into the beach while Orv secured the rope around a cleat on the front of the float. With almost no breeze, he wasn't worried about his plane drifting away. If the winds picked up, he would drop a second anchor.

"Come join me," said Kevin. "I just ordered, and my clients are looking pretty cozy over there. I don't think I'm in a hurry."

Orv glanced over at one of the umbrella-covered tables set up on the beach. A man in his early sixties was sitting dangerously close to a beautiful, late twenties blonde. They only had eyes for each other. He laughed as he followed Kevin up towards the bar, "Yeah, you've got some time."

Orv ordered his conch sandwich and considered another beer but decided on water instead. Everybody in the restaurant had watched him pilot the plane in, so drinking was risky. The last time he had flown into the Lorelei for lunch, the tall, sultry bartender he knew as Taltura had delivered his beer to him in a tall coke cup with a lid and a straw. He looked but didn't see her working the bar.

Kevin and Orv sat and chatted. When Kevin asked him what he was up to, he said he was retired. He was just heading down to Key West to see an old friend. Kevin had heard rumors that Orv was flying contraband but didn't question him. He accepted the retirement story then updated his friend on his wife and kids. They ate, told stories, laughed, and then Orv paid the check. They promised to get together soon.

Walking back to the beach, Orv quietly chuckled at an elderly couple who were taking pictures of each other standing by the planes. After pulling the anchor, Kevin helped Orv turn the Beaver around, facing her away from the beach. Glancing one last time at Kevin's unlikely couple at the table, Orv didn't figure his buddy was going anywhere soon. It was just another afternoon at the Lorelei.

Somewhere over Georgia, Alice set her book in her lap, laid her head back against the seat, and closed her eyes. Her thoughts were of him, her ex-husband, Orv. She remembered him coming home from the war, shattered and broken, both in body and spirit. His recovery was slow, but after a few years, he was almost completely recovered, and he became determined to return to flying. He received his commercial pilot's license and found a job with a little cargo airline. The only thing that bothered her about his job was the hours; most cargo flies at night. He flew three to four times a week, almost always returning home as she was leaving for work.

But they had a good life. They rented a little house in Opa-locka and made the most out of the time they did have together. Orv initially flew from Miami to Tampa, Jacksonville, and Atlanta as the co-pilot on a small Metroliner, but as his hours and experience grew, he moved to the captain's seat and then on to bigger planes. After accepting an offer from a competing airline, he started flying south into the Caribbean. He delivered newspapers and produce to the islands that she only saw on maps or in magazines. Within a few years, he was flying co-pilot on a 737 and working on his type rating so he could move to the left seat.

She remembered him feeling guilty about his small paychecks, always promising her he would make more soon. "One day," he always said, "our ship will come in." When it did, she would be able quit her job at the Sheriff's Department and go to law school. She told him she didn't care, she liked her job and was even questioning if she was still interested in becoming a lawyer. She wasn't sure it was still her dream.

Thinking back, she realized for the first time that it was probably the pressure to make more money that got him into the Jamaica situation. His desire to fulfill his promises to her likely caused one of their more significant life changes.

She remembered how excited he was, coming home one morning after a regular flight to Jamaica and back. "There are planes for sale, cheap!" he enthusiastically told her. Six older de Havilland Dash Eights sat unused at Norman Manley International in Kingston. They had been seized by the government due to unpaid taxes and the government wanted to sell them quickly.

"It's the start of something big," he told her. "It's a sign!"

She pointed out the obvious: they didn't have enough money to buy a second car. How were they going to buy six airplanes? And the big obstacle: he was a good pilot, but he knew nothing about running an airline. Orv, however, was undeterred. He was excited to take the risk; to build an airline and get rich. When he should have been sleeping, he instead made coffee and filled pages of his notebook with thoughts and ideas. He made hundreds of phone calls, he sent emails, and asked her to drop letters to New York and Boston in the mail for him. She had never seen him so driven. She couldn't help to be excited with him, and for him.

As the plan evolved, it took on some interesting twists and turns. He met a bright, young Wall Street guy from New York named Charles Tinsley who claimed to have access to millions of dollars of capital and could get millions more with a little work. Tinsley's plan wasn't to buy the planes and operate an airline; his twist was a little different. His plan, as Alice understood it, was to talk the Jamaican government into selling them the airplanes but also financing them, forming a partnership.

Orv and Tinsley would set up a maintenance and hub facility, hire management, pilots and ground crews, build routes, and then win contracts to fly the same cargo that Orv had been hauling around the islands for a few years. Tinsley's plan to get the cargo contacts was easy enough. They would bid so low that the other operators couldn't compete. The airline might lose money for a year, but down the road, their competitors would be either out of the market or out of business. Then the airline would raise rates because they would be the only game in town.

It then evolved into even more of a shell game. When everything was set up, just before their first flight, they would sell the entire operation to an investment group in the States. "A turnkey airline," Tinsley called it. "All licensed, contracted, set up, and ready to fly, an investor's wet dream." Their efforts would make them rich. It was a scheme to make a fortune that almost couldn't go awry.

Alice cautioned Orv to be careful. She didn't completely trust the young, slick equity trader from New York. She remembered her father's advice. If it seemed too good to be true, it probably was. But Orv convinced her that the deal wasn't that risky to them. They would have no money invested into the venture, only time. The new corporation that Tinsley set up would pay Orv a salary similar to what he was currently making until they sold out, then he would never need a salary again. And if the entire thing failed, Orv could get a job with another airline. He would keep plodding along, earning his hours, and working towards better pay with a passenger airline.

He was so excited, she couldn't say no, even while all the warning bells rang in her head. She gave him her blessing, she told him to be careful, and then she told him they were going to have a baby.

***

After taxiing out more than a half mile, Orv radioed his intentions to anybody who might be listening then turned back towards the island and advanced the throttle.

He was airborne and cleared the island by 500 feet, waggling his wings to his buddy Kevin as he passed over the beach restaurant. He crossed the island and banked to the right, looking down at Catarina Carol Gardens, a beautiful park named after his old fishing buddy Jim's late wife. Turning southwest, he followed the highway at an altitude of just two thousand feet.

The calm water below him was absolutely beautiful, a turquoise color that looked incredibly inviting. On days like this, he was convinced that he had the best job in the world. His "office" had an amazing one-hundred-and-eighty-degree view of some of the most stunning scenery in the world. The green hues of the islands seemed to contrast perfectly with the water and the blue skies. Crossing the Overseas Highway again at Long Key, he turned a bit to the south to parallel the Seven Mile Bridge. Traffic across the bridge was bumper to bumper in both directions. He looked but couldn't see another aircraft for twenty miles. There was zero traffic at two thousand feet; he had made the right decision to fly.

Flying had always been the right decision. The world seemed quiet when he was in the air. A few thousand feet above the earth's surface, there were no screaming kids, no TVs with loud hosts yelling their opinions about politics, sports, or whatnot. Everything was peaceful when he flew. Even in a raging storm, it seemed quiet and tranquil compared to the noise on the ground. He remembered a line from a Sunny Jim song: "Let the rats run the race, I'm going to go my own pace." He looked down at the rats on the bridge and smiled while wondering where they were going to park all those vehicles on the tiny islands at the end of the road.

At No Name Key, he contacted Key West approach, who turned him due west to keep him far out of the traffic patterns for both Key West International and Naval Air Station Key West. He stated his intentions, to land on the east side of Fleming Key in an area known as the Garrison Bight Channel. The tower approved his plan, advising him to watch for helicopter traffic in and out of Coast Guard Station Key West. Five seconds later, the Coast Guard radioed that they had no inbound or outbound traffic at the moment.

The water below him was calm and flat. The winds were remarkably light for the time of day. He lined up on the channel between Fleming Key to his west and the large boat mooring field to the east. There were a couple of boats transiting the channel creating a bit of an obstacle course on his "runway." He never understood why seaplanes didn't have big airhorns like the semi-trucks on the freeway. He saw a man in a dinghy look over his shoulder then quickly turn to dart out of his way. A thirty-foot sailboat coming out of the anchorage was his last challenge. The sailor at the helm either didn't want to yield or was too busy mixing a drink to notice there was a plane coming right at him.

At the last moment, Orv leveled the plane and passed over the sailboat, probably giving their crew quite a shock. He then pushed the yoke forward to dive steeply towards the water to land in a much abbreviated but still doable stretch of water. He sat her down a little harder than he would have liked to, but the Beaver settled in and slowed quickly with fifty yards to spare off the Coast Guard Heliport. As he turned to his left to taxi, he noticed the old seaplane ramps that led from the water to the tarmac. He smiled; they took him back to a time when the Coast Guard operated Martin P5Ms and Grumman Gooses. He wondered if they had ever operated the huge Grumman Albatross out of Key West.

He taxied past the heliport and the rows of base housing on the spit that created Garrison Bight. At Trumbo point, he turned towards the long boat dock that jutted to the north. Owned by his friend Giles, he had been told he was always welcome to tie up there. He cut the engine, crawled down onto the float, and stepped onto the deck with a mooring line in hand just as the float nudged up against the newly rebuilt dock.

He carefully secured the plane, then grabbed his backpack before locking the plane's doors. He wasn't concerned about somebody stealing his plane. There were only a handful of people on the island who could start the old Beaver, let alone fly her. He was more concerned about returning to find some drunk tourist sitting in it, pretending he was shooting down enemy fighter planes. Or worse, finding somebody who was passed out in their own puke after finding a handy place to sleep off a bad drunk. It was Key West after all.

If Giles had been home, he would have come out to greet him. Not seeing the stout little Frenchman, he walked off the dock, past the vacant swimming pool, and into the home's breezeway. Several bicycles leaned against the side of the house. He picked one that had air in both tires, knowing that Giles would be happy to loan it to him, if he were here. Throwing a leg over the top bar, he pushed off and headed towards some of his old haunts for a cold beer. He hadn't spent any time on the island in more than a year. It would be fun to see who was around.

***

As her flight descended toward Miami, Alice continued to think about those crazy, wonderful, horrible years with Orv. She remembered how excited they were to be having a baby, and at the same time, the business venture in Jamaica seemed to be going very well. Despite some early bumps, the Jamaican government was on board, which helped in a number of ways. It also lightened the number of bribes that needed to be given to get things done. Bribery on the little island nation was simply a way of life; it was part of doing business. While it was considered an illegal and taboo practice in the U.S., it was a budget-line item in many parts of the world. Grease the right palm and a license application or a building permit slipped right through the system. Moving your business needs to the top of the bureaucratic stack simply saved time and money.

When Orv was home, they worked to turn the spare room into a nursery as Alice's tummy grew. They shared the excitement when they felt the baby kick and as the various pieces and parts of the airline plans came to fruition.

Alice's first inclination that anything was amiss came when Charles Tinsley organized a dinner so the investors from New York could meet Orv and his wife. The hair on the back of her neck stood up when she met Vince and Frankie DiPiero at a nice restaurant on South Beach. The two brothers, who Charles said represented their family's investments, looked and acted like Jersey mobsters. They were polite and well-mannered, but after Vince drank more than his share of scotch, he started getting mouthy and complaining about the outrageous amount of bribe money they were fronting to get the permits and licenses to operate in the Caribbean. He talked about "going down there and knocking some heads together." Then he got belligerent and racist.

The next day at her office, she ran their names through the system and found that years earlier, Vince had some minor brushes with the law: assault and battery and petty theft. Frankie looked like a choirboy with not even a speeding ticket tied to his name. Despite their relatively clean records, she knew they were dirty. Orv had left the dinner with the same impressions, but he reminded her that in just a few months, they would complete the deal, sell the airline, and be done with the DiPiero brothers and Charles Tinsley forever. Alice crossed her fingers and prayed that her intuitions were wrong. She told herself that just because they were Italians from New Jersey, it didn't mean they were part of the mob. She was wrong.

Forty-seven days later, their daughter, Jessica, was born and immediately rushed into the neonatal intensive care unit. Two months after that, as the World Trade Center towers collapsed, Jessica died from cystic fibrosis.

The world was in shock, the financial markets closed, the FAA grounded all civilian air traffic in the U.S. Travel, and tourism became nearly non-existent. Charles Tinsley, who had an office on the 94th floor of the World Trade Center's North Tower, died in the attacks. The FBI showed up at Orv and Alice's home asking if they knew the whereabouts of the DiPiero brothers, who had suddenly disappeared. The investment group that was lined up to purchase the airline pulled out of the transaction. Orv and Alice's world fell apart before their eyes.

Orv received a letter from the Jamaican government telling him that they held him personally and criminally responsible for the failed airline transaction. If he ever returned to their country, he would be imprisoned. Under pressure from the Jamaicans, the U.S. Federal Aviation Administration launched an investigation into the scheme. They couldn't find enough evidence to recommend legal action to the Attorney General. Instead, they decided to hand down the largest penalty they could. They revoked his commercial pilot's license.

All Alice could do was sit in their bedroom and cry over the death of their baby. Orv tried but couldn't console her. She shut down emotionally, then he opened a bottle and crawled inside.

CHAPTER THREE

Little had changed since his last trip to the island, he thought to himself as he weaved his bike through the mid-afternoon tourists and traffic. He had some time to kill before his meeting at the Green Parrot and felt the need to see some friendly faces. He thought it would be fun to seek out some of his old friends, people he hadn't seen in a while, but he wasn't sure where he might find them. A safe bet was the Smokin' Tuna or Turtle Kraals, but they would both be starting to get their daily deluge of happy hour tourists. He decided on Blue Heaven, a little restaurant off Thomas Street.

The traffic in town and the amount of gawking, drunk tourists were thicker than he remembered as he carefully navigated Truman Avenue. After nearly running over a lady who jumped out in the street in front of him to get a picture of her husband standing in front of the lighthouse, he made it to the Heaven. He leaned his bike on the fence and found an outside table.

Looking around, he didn't see a soul he knew. A cute, twenty-something waitress took his beer order and quickly brought it to him. As he enjoyed his cold beer in the shade, two roosters engaged in a minor squabble below his table. The waitress reappeared to shoo them away from him and apologized for their behavior. Orv just gave a smile and took another sip of his beer.

After finishing the beer and paying his tab, he retrieved his trusty steed, then rode one block up and two blocks over to get to the Green Parrot. The Parrot was one of the older bars in town and it certainly showed its age. Being just a little out of the regular tourist area, it drew in more locals than the bars over on Duval, but over the years, it had also become a destination for the flocks of visitors from the north. Glancing around as he walked in, he didn't see Angel and his sidekick/bodyguard, so he took a seat at the bar next to two tourists and ordered another beer. The man sitting next to him asked him if he was a local. Orv guessed he must have had the look of a Conch.

"No," he replied. "I'm just down from Miami for the night."

The two guys introduced themselves as Dave and Eric. They were in town from Charlotte to do a little fishing and chase some tail. They asked if Orv knew the best place to find some action. He laughed. "The sure bet is to find a couple of hookers, but you boys don't need hookers in Key West. Just go troll the bars on Duval around midnight. You'll find plenty of drunken out-of-towners who will fit the bill."

A slap on the back got his attention. He turned to see Angel's grumpy-looking tag-a-long doing his best to appear mean and menacing. He didn't say anything; he just pointed with his thumb over his shoulder. Turning, Orv could see Angel sitting at a corner table.

"You boys have fun," he said to his new friends at the bar. "Be careful, the Keys can bite back if you let your guard down."

Angel's thug followed him towards the table then stood nearby as Orv took a chair across from the Puerto Rican. Angel was an interesting character. He was probably in his early forties and was all about the show. He wore expensive jewelry and kept his hair long and slicked back into a ponytail that dropped below his collar. He did his best to look and act like the Puerto Rican version of Snoop Dog, slouching in his chair and intentionally slurring his speech. He paid to have an overweight brute follow him around while trying his best to look tough. The guy was probably a friend he had grown up with in the barrios of Puerto Rico. His presence had never bothered or intimidated Orv.

Orv set his beer on the table then leaned across to shake Angel's hand. "How are you, Angel? It's been awhile."

Angel smiled. "Life is good, and it is good to see you, my friend."

Orv was relieved. The tone of the meeting was friendly and light. He never knew what to expect when dealing with Angel. He heard through the rumor mill, not long after he started flying for Angel, that the previous pilot had lost his life because he had been pinching some of the goods for his own profit. Orv didn't want anything to do with the pot he flew, but he also knew that a simple misunderstanding or a miscalculation could cost him his life.

"What can I do for you?" Orv asked, getting right to the heart of the meeting. The less time he spent in a public place talking with a known drug lord, the better.

Angel sipped his mojito while staring at the pilot, seemingly sizing him up, but Orv felt the pause was more for dramatic effect than any other reason. "An opportunity has presented itself," he said finally. "We are expanding into the upper Keys and maybe even onto the mainland." Angel gave Orv a smile before he took another drink. "Miami isn't out of the question."

Orv was surprised. The expansion he spoke of represented a lot of territory and a lot of weed. "You're jumping fences?" he asked, using drug runner slang. Dogs that jumped their fences was a term to describe dealers who crossed into another dealer's territory. Everybody knew that the islands below Matacumbe were Angel's territory.

As long as he didn't sell above Islamorada, everybody left him alone.

Angel's eyes widened slightly at the pilot's question, but he calmly replied, "I have a new partner who has been testing the markets up north. Nobody seems to care that we are moving towards the mainland."

Orv did his best to quell his laugh. He had heard that the "new partner" was an old beach cowboy named John who had been slumming around the Keys for years. The guy was a fellow Vietnam vet who was a little off center and a little half gone. He rented rafts down on Smathers Beach and sold joints out of a cigar box until he talked Angel into a bigger deal. Now he was selling ganja where he shouldn't be and had convinced Angel that nobody cared. He knew somebody cared. Drug dealers had mouths to feed and wives to keep happy. He didn't guess this "new opportunity" was going to turn out well for Angel or John.

"How does this involve me?" asked Orv.

"We're going to need a lot more supply," replied Angel. "For now, we'll keep our routes and plans in place, only delivering to the Lower Keys. We can move it north by car. But we're going to need to at least double the flights."

Running his hand across the stubble on his chin, Orv grimaced. Double the flights meant double the risk of getting caught. Refusing to fly would likely mean getting fired, and drug runners didn't like having disgruntled ex-employees running around. If he quit, he'd probably need to move somewhere far away to be safe.

Up until this moment, flying for Angel had been a pretty good deal. It paid well, and the geography of the Lower Keys, laid out like the world's largest maze, made it an easy place to play hide and seek with the authorities while moving drugs.

Just after he had started flying, he and boat captain Ken Hopkins had devised a plan, a code that had worked out very well. By texting a single letter of the alphabet and the abbreviated day of the week, "RTH" for example, Orv and Ken knew exactly when and where to meet. The first letter indicated the spot, one of twenty-four they had agreed upon. The day of the week was intentionally three days forward, so Thursday really meant Sunday. "RTH" indicated that, on the following Sunday, they would meet in the northern straits of Cudjoe Key. The only constant was the time of day. Orv timed his flights so he could land on the water during daylight hours and still make it back to Miami before dark. He always landed in the Keys about 3pm.

Orv decided to play along for the moment, to act as if doubling the flights meant nothing to him. He could decide later if he wanted to quit and disappear. "If you can get the supply to the Bahamas, I can get it to the Keys." To further calm Angel, he tossed out, "I'll fly every day if you have the need."

Angel smiled. "I knew you'd take care of business if I asked." He reached into his pocket and pulled out a folded wad of bills and tossed it across the table. "Here's a little bonus for your excellent work. And I'm giving you an extra five Gs per flight, a raise for being our employee of the month."

With that, Angel pushed back his chair and stood up. "You can pay for my drink," he said with a smile. "I heard you just got a fat bonus." He tipped his head towards his muscle and then pointed at Orv, saying, "Be good" as he walked out of the bar.

Orv slipped the wad of bills into his shirt pocket without looking at it or counting it. He was sure it was generous.

***

On the cab ride from the airport to her condo, Alice scolded herself for once again allowing Jessica and Orv back into her conscious mind. Jessica never went away; every waking moment, the grief felt like a sword stabbing her in the heart. It never got better, it never got easier, but over time, she became numb and desensitized to the pain. Orv was another story; the guilt and heartache she felt for him was easier to bury. After Jessica's death and the fiasco in Jamaica, Orv fell into a depression. He was like a bird without its wings. He stood on the ground and looked at the other birds flying around and had no idea what to do.

The only thing Orv had ever wanted to do is to fly. The FAA pulling his commercial ticket was like they had pulled out his heart. Between the failed venture, the loss of his license, and the death of his daughter, he fell into a such a deep depression that Alice wasn't sure he would survive. He took a night security job at the Seminole Hard Rock Casino to help pay the rent, but he looked and acted like a zombie wandering the earth without a soul. The light in his eyes was gone and Alice was too mired in her own depression to help him. They drifted apart while sleeping in the same bed.

She found by suppressing both her ex-husband and beautiful little daughter's memories, she could function and live a fairly normal life. But every now and then, something like the man in the exit row of her flight reminded her of them. If she wasn't careful, she would find herself mired in weeks or even months of depression.

Work seemed to help. She knew she could bury herself in her work and push both of them back into the dark recesses of her brain. It was late, and she knew she should go home, but she knew what thoughts and memories were there waiting for her there. She asked the cab driver to take her to her office in West Palm Beach. There, she would be able to work for several hours, and when she got home, she could collapse and hopefully find sleep aided by exhaustion. She was angry for letting the two people she loved the most back into her thoughts. The only therapy that had worked in the past was several weeks of fourteen- to sixteen-hour days, immersing herself deep into her work, thinking of nothing but the project at hand until sleep came.

After tipping the driver, she pulled her suitcase up to her third-floor office, surprising the janitor. She went to work on her new project, figuring out how to stop the flow of drugs into the Lower Keys by boat and airplane.

***

Orv walked his bike a block over to Mr. Z's for a Philly cheesesteak and a cold beer. Waiting to cross Duval Street, he ran into his old friend, Ed Atz. Ed was just one of the many colorful full-time residences of the Conch Republic. He and his wife Susan had been around the island for as long as he had been coming there. He walked every day to stay in shape and always pushed his two dogs, Ella and Tessa, around in a stroller. Ed and his dogs went out every afternoon in search of good live music and a Coors Light or two. He seemed to know every local and many of the tourists by name.

Orv invited Ed to join him for a beer and a bite, but Ed politely declined, saying he had to get home to his wife. "She's always worried that I might die on one of my walks and nobody will notice," he said with a laugh.

After enjoying a cheesesteak sandwich, Orv was ready to go find a place to spend the night. Giles, his friend with the home on Trumbo Point, would likely offer him a room, or he could sleep in his plane. He always kept a blanket and pad rolled up and stashed in back, just in case.

Giles Boutier was an interesting character, a fixture in the Keys. He was the son of a wealthy French industrialist who had broken away from his family's business and spent most of his life sailing around the world. Now in his sixties, he had more or less settled in Key West. Over the years, he had become another interesting actor in one of the country's largest melodramas, a day in the life of Key West.

Leaving Mr. Z's, Orv found himself drawn next door by the sound of familiar music coming from Willie T's. Peeking around the corner, he recognized the musician but couldn't remember his name. He played an acoustic guitar to a nearly packed house. Spotting a table near the sidewalk, he decided to take a seat, hear some good music, and consider the evening's lodging options over another cold beer.

Orv had seen the singer several times and always found his lyrics to be catchy, sometimes incredibly thought-provoking, at times just downright funny. He seemed to sing mostly drinking songs, which the crowd really liked. He sang a song about Belize, a country Orv had always been interested to see. As the man played on, Orv wondered if he could make a living flying tourists around the islands and cayes of the little Central American country. It might not be as profitable as flying dope in the Keys, but it would certainly be less stressful.

He had often dreamed of packing his few possessions in his plane and flying south to some other destination. He envisioned a beach on a small protected bay with a longboat dock, his plane tied up, resting on the emerald green waters. In his dream, he sat in the shade of a coconut tree near his little shack, watching pelicans diving on bait as a soft trade wind kept him cool.

There was no reason to stay in Florida, doing what he did. He had given enough and had done his fair share many times over. But he continued to fly contraband and he continued to pay his penance.

"Where are these drunk women you told us about?" The voice behind him shook him from his island dream. Turning, he saw the two guys from Charlotte he had spoken to at the Parrot.

"Get over here and sit down," Orv ordered with a bit of a growl.

Eric and Dave stumbled around to the entrance and made their way to his table. "Look at the two of you," said Orv with a disgusted tone. "You went out and got yourselves all drunked-up. How do you expect to pick up women if you're in this kind of shape?"

The two young men started pointing and blaming each other. "I don't want to hear it," said Orv. "You two need to go find your hotel room and sleep it off. Then come back tomorrow and act like you're on a mission. I told you Key West would bite you in the ass if you weren't careful." Surprisingly, they stood, thanked him, and wandered off. He actually believed they were heading for their hotel, unless they got distracted along the way, which was highly likely on Duval Street.

"You're a good mentor," said the woman at the table next to him. Orv turned to see a pretty lady, about ten years younger than himself, he guessed.

"I'm just trying to keep the streets of Key West safe from North Carolina drunks," he said with a laugh.

She smiled a pretty smile. "All of us drunks from Virginia appreciate it. I'm Kelly," she said as she extended her hand towards him. They shook hands, then Kelly stood and moved to his table, bringing her cocktail with her. Her friends at the other table didn't say a word; they barely glanced when she moved to his table.

"Hi, Kelly, I'm Orv."

"What brings you to Key West, Orv?" she asked.

He chuckled. "I flew down here for a ten-minute meeting."

"You paid the airfare to fly down here for a ten-minute meeting?" she asked incredulously.

"Well, no. I have my own plane, so it cost much more than an airline ticket."

"Wow," she said, acting impressed. "What kind of plane do you have?"

Orv suddenly wished he hadn't brought it up. "I have a de Havilland Beaver on floats."

"A seaplane?" replied Kelly. "I'm impressed. Where is it?"

"It's tied up at a friend's house off of Trumbo Point."

She smiled. "You should take me for a ride. I'll bet the lights of Key West are beautiful at night."

Orv laughed. "They are—incredible to see as they appear on the horizon when you fly north from Cuba. It doesn't matter how many times you've flown from Cuba to Key West at night, it's always a welcome sight. On a clear night, you can see the glow on the horizon first, then, like the sunrise, the glow gets brighter and brighter until the lights crest the horizon and lead you home."

Kelly put her hand on her chest. "Oh my God, you're a romantic."

Orv blushed while grumbling, "I'm a pilot, not a romantic."

From the stage, the guitar player told the story of how he spent a month in Montana and how cold it was there. Then he said he was going to play a song he had written during that month called Montana Moon. Kelly stood without a word, took Orv by the hand, and led him to the dance floor. It would have been more awkward to argue than to follow the pretty woman who had a tight grip on his hand.

That dance and the look in Kelly's eyes ignited a feeling that Orv hadn't felt in a very long time. He sensed a wildness, a devil-may-care attitude that felt good; it seemed like he was eighteen again with a pretty young thing in his arms and a pocket full of cash. The world felt full of possibilities. They danced every dance until the singer finished playing, then they started drinking and dancing their way up Duval Street. Walking arm in arm, they were having fun being drunk and silly. At Irish Kevin's Bar, she surprised him with a kiss, and at the Hog's Breath Saloon, they found a table in the back and made out like teenagers.

Kelly kept ordering drinks. Orv kept paying for them out of the fat wad of cash Angel had given him. He was having a ball.

***

Alice woke, raised her head, and realized she had fallen asleep at her desk. She looked at the clock and saw it was almost six thirty in the morning. She had called a staff meeting at eight. There was no way she could get home, get ready, and get back to the office by then. Fortunately, her suitcase stood next to her desk and the second-floor restrooms had a shower for those who worked out in the tiny exercise room adjacent to the breakroom.

By seven thirty, she had made herself reasonably presentable, wearing the same outfit she had worn two days earlier. She still had thirty minutes to put her final thoughts together for the meeting. She sent a text to her assistant, asking her to stop by McDonald's for one of those sausage egg breakfast things.

She had just enough time to chomp down her breakfast before the meeting started, then she strode into the conference room with a confident and determined look on her face. She was ready to do battle with the drug smugglers in the Keys.

Everybody stopped talking when she walked into the room. She picked up a remote control on the table and pressed a button, bringing up a detailed map of the southern tip of Florida on the large screen behind her. "Good morning," she said with a blunt, businesslike tone. "As you know, I have just returned from a series of meetings in Washington. Director Campbell has asked us to change our focus. Our group will be assisting the Coast Guard, the TSA, and local law enforcement in stopping the flow of drugs by aircraft and boat into this area."

She could see the looks of disbelief on her staff's faces. The map before them represented the southern portion of the Everglades National Park, Florida Bay, and the sprawling Florida Keys. It was more than a thousand square miles of some of the most remote and least patrolled areas in the United States. The entire area was accessible by only two highways. Land masses within the map area, those large enough to be named, numbered in the thousands.

After giving her group of fifteen people a moment to consider the enormity of the task, but before they could start arguing about the impossible mission she was proposing, she pushed a button, bringing up the second slide. The projection on the wall showed the Lower Keys, everything east of Seven Mile Bridge. "We are going to start here, we are going to clean up the Lower Keys first, then we'll expand our operations to Florida Bay and then the Everglades."

She watched their faces turn from questioning and doubtful to confident. It was a trick she had learned years earlier at the Sheriff's Department. Show them a

monumental goal—"We are going to build a skyscraper"—
and then ask them to instead focus on the objective. "But
today, we're going to start by each of you laying one brick
of the foundation."

Switching to the next slide, a list of tasks with her
team names next to each appeared. "Johnny, I want you to
contact the Monroe County Sheriff's office and the Police
Department in Key West. You will be our liaison with them.
I've heard they haven't been very cooperative with us in
the past, so you'll have a big task of building a working
partnership with them. Angela, you will reach out to the
Coast Guard. We'll start at the top; Admiral Terrill's office
then work our way down to Station Key West. Kali will
continue to work with the TSA. Mark, I want you to
contact the Florida Fish and Wildlife Conservation
Commission. Their help will be vital. Nobody knows those
Keys like they do. Paul, the Navy is right up your alley. I
think we may have drugs being smuggled in by naval
personnel. I don't have anything to back that up, but you
will reach out to NAS Key West to both coordinate their
resources and to see what we can do to assist them in
stopping any breaches they may have."

Once she finished the lengthy list of duties, she
gave them all three days to make their contacts and be
ready to report back. "We'll meet here again on Wednesday
morning, I have already sent you meeting invites. I want
each of you to detail your conversations and be ready to
talk about any challenges we may have with the
organizations assigned to you."

She paused for a moment, simply for effect.
"Understand, we are going to war against a very organized
but incredibly fragmented group of people who are as
motivated at continuing their profitable businesses as we
are at stopping them. This has never been an easy job, and I
don't expect this to be an easy mission, but never before
has the agency given us such a laser focus. For the first

time ever, we only need to work on a thousand-square-mile area, and I've narrowed that down to only two hundred square miles to start. Let's stop the flow of drugs into the Lower Keys, then let's chase the drug runners as they move north. We'll stop them dead when they hit the mainland with help from local law enforcement." She stood for a moment before continuing, "See me if you have any questions; otherwise, have your reports ready for Wednesday's meeting."

She turned and walked out of the room. She couldn't help but smile at her confidence and the way she had controlled the room.

***

He was cold. Orv opened his eyes just enough to see that he was lying on the floor and that he was naked. A shirt lay within his reach; it wasn't his, but he pulled it over his shoulders to try to get warm. He couldn't muster the energy or the motivation to move to the bed that stood just five feet away. His head hurt, his stomach hurt. He laid his head back on the hard, cold floor and tried to get some more sleep.

Shivering on the floor, hoping to fall back to sleep, he tried to remember where he was and how he had gotten there. He recalled drinking, dancing, and a lot of laughing with the pretty woman from Virginia. He heard a snore and a rustle of sheets above him. He guessed it was the woman from the night before. They had made a pact to hit every bar on the island in one night, an impossible task in a week, but from the pain he felt, they must have made a pretty good effort.

Finally, the cold he absorbed from the floor overcame his hangover and lack of sleep. He crawled to the bed and looked over the edge. A familiar face stared back at him. "Whatcha doing down there?" she asked.

"I don't remember," he truthfully replied.

She tossed back the covers, exposing her naked figure and silently inviting him to join her. He crawled onto the bed and lay with his back to her. She snuggled up to him, spooning him. Her soft, warm body, the comfy bed, and the covers over him felt wonderful. He fell into a heavy sleep.

***

Alice was starting to grasp the enormity of the task she faced. On paper, the Lower Keys wasn't a big area. There was one international airport, one Naval Air Station, a Coast Guard Station, and one cruise ship dock. There were thirty-five thousand residences in the area, and five thousand military personnel. But the little area played host to a million and a half visitors each year. They arrived by car, boat, ship, and airplane. She made a note to find the number of boats and aircraft registered in the Keys.

Retrieving her map of the islands, she had hoped to estimate the miles of shoreline they needed to control but gave up after a minute. The number of points of entry, the public and private docks, accessible beaches, and usable shoreline was incalculable. Add to that the thousands of little islands and inlets that only hunters, fisherman, and manatee knew about, and it was clear there was no way, even if she brought in the entire U.S. Military, to patrol every point of entry in the area.

Stopping and searching every boat and aircraft that came into the area was also impossible. That would number in the hundreds or even thousands a day and require a massive amount of law enforcement personnel to conduct that many stops. There was also the consideration of the constitutionality of stopping every craft that crossed some line on the map.

She would need to find a way to infiltrate the drug runners' communications and plans. She needed to understand more about the nuts and bolts of flying in and out of the Keys from both foreign and domestic points of origination. She wanted to understand how an aircraft or boat might be tracked after returning from Cuba or the Bahamas, or even Bimini. How did they avoid U.S. Customs? What were the normal communication procedures and how did the druggies skirt around them?

She briefly thought of her ex-husband, Orv. He would be an incredible resource to her if she knew where to find him, and if he didn't cause her so much mental chaos. She pushed him to the back of her mind again and started searching for a contact with the Coast Guard or the FAA.

The first of her team to visit her with problems was Special Agent Johnny Reno. She had known Johnny and worked alongside him for several years. They enjoyed a good working relationship spanning back to her days at Dade County. "I called the Monroe County Sheriff's Department and spoke with a woman in charge of their Narcotics division, Deputy Eubanks. You were right," he said with a grimace. "We have some bridge building to do down there."

"How bad is it?" asked Alice.

Johnny shook his head. "It seems your predecessor watched too many movies. He had a reputation of stepping into the middle of their investigations and stating that we were in charge. Because we were a federal agency, we assumed we knew more than the locals. She basically told me to buzz off and stay out of their county. She was polite, but the message was clear."

Alice muttered a little cussword under her breath as she looked at her calendar. "What are you doing tomorrow?" she asked Reno.

"I've got a pretty busy day," he replied.

"Me too," said Alice. "Let's reschedule everything and leave here at eight. See if Deputy, what did you say her name was?"

"Eubanks," answered Reno.

"See if Deputy Eubanks will have lunch with us and invite the sheriff along too if he's available. Find out what you can about the two of them. Leave your suit and tie at home, slacks and a golf shirt. We're going to look casual, approachable, and friendly." She returned to the map on her desk then looked up with an idea as he left her office. "Johnny, as long as we're going as far as Plantation Key, let's reach out to the Key West Police Department too. The Chief used to be a guy named Don Brewer. He was a reasonable guy. We worked together on a joint investigation several years ago. See if he or his successor is available for a quick meeting."

Johnny nodded and left her office. Getting face time with the locals was the right decision, the right move, but why did it have to be tomorrow? He thought of all the things he had hoped to accomplish and the meetings he needed to postpone and reschedule as he walked back to his office. He grimaced while remembering his previous boss. Alice was a breath of fresh air in the department. His personal satisfaction with his job had risen immensely since she had taken the role. And after all, a day in the Keys wasn't a bad day at work.

**

The light of mid-morning shined through the blinds when Orv woke a second time. His head still hurt, and he needed some coffee, a few aspirin, and a couple of beers. Rolling over, he found he was alone in the bed, and after a moment of listening, it seemed he was alone in the hotel room. Crawling out of bed, he found his underwear on the floor and struggled to balance as he slipped them on. He went to the bathroom where he found a note on the mirror. It read: *"Thanks for the fun night, Orv. Maybe we'll run into each other again someday. XXOO, Kelly."*

It was clear what the note from the stranger really said: *"I had a fun night, now get out of my room."* Standing in front of the mirror, he hardly recognized his reflection. Even though he had spent the night in the arms of a younger, pretty woman, that morning, he felt old. His hair was disheveled, his beard was gray and unruly; even the sunken divot on his chest and the old scar that covered it looked wrinkled and gray.

After splashing water in his face and doing the best he could to clean himself up without taking a shower, he wandered through the room looking for his belongings. His shorts lay on the floor; he checked, and his wallet was still in the back pocket. The remains of the big wad of cash from Angel was in the front right pocket. His right flipflop was near the TV, but his left one was missing. He found his shirt and his hat, then finally found his missing flipflop under some covers that had been dumped off the bed.

Orv laughed as he left the room and found his way to the lobby. He didn't remember where he was. The interior of the hotel looked like every other mid-priced hotel in the area. Stepping out the front door, he was relieved to see the water and a familiar little bar by the pier. He knew right where he was and where to find the beer he so desperately needed. He squinted in the sunlight and reached for the Maui Jim sunglasses that he kept in his shirt pocket. They were missing. After a beer or two, he would find a new pair.

The little bar was almost empty except for three tourists in the corner, an old drunk at the bar, and the bartender who sat on a stool at the end of the bar picking his guitar. He took a stool a few over from the solo guy at the bar and ordered a beer. When the bartender delivered it to him, Orv looked at the guy, who looked back at him with a questioning expression. They recognized each other, but neither could put a finger on why. Without a word, the bartender turned and went to check on the three out of towners, then he went back to his stool and his guitar. Orv stole glances at him as he quietly practiced a song, mostly humming but sometimes singing a few lines.

When the singer/bartender delivered his second beer, it struck him where he had seen Orv before. He leaned in close. "You're a pilot."

Orv was surprised but nodded.

"You fly a floatplane. I think you know my friend Ken Hopkins."

With the name, Orv knew exactly who the bartender was. He was the younger man who was on the fishing boat the other day, the guy who had accompanied Ken out to the drop zone off No Name Key. Orv didn't want to say much, but in an attempt to be cordial, asked, "Did Ken hire a mate?"

"Ken retired," said the bartender. "I'm taking over for him. I heard we'll be seeing each other more often now." He held out his hand and said, "I'm Jack."

Orv took Jack's hand while saying, "You can call me Bob."

"Nice to meet you, Bob," said the bartender. "How long have you been flying for this organization?"

Orv took a sip of his beer then narrowed his eyes. "I don't want to be rude, but the less we know about each other, the safer we each are if someone gets in trouble."

Jack was new to the game, having only recently been recruited to drive the boat after Hopkins' retirement. Jack was a first world refugee, a guy who had escaped the corporate world and moved to the Keys. He was trying to make ends meet by bartending while trying to play his guitar around town. He hoped to build a career writing and singing songs. In the meantime, an old high school buddy had gotten him hooked up with Angel. He was excited to start making some serious money by ferrying a couple of big bags of pot a time or two a week.

"That makes sense," said Jack to Orv. "I'll see you the day after tomorrow."

"Friday?" asked Orv.

"I got a text this morning arranging a run. I sent you a code for confirmation. Did you get it?"

Orv took a sip of his beer then pulled his phone out of his pocket. It was dead. He cussed under his breath, still not sure he wanted to double or triple his number of flights. "Not yet," he grumbled. "I'll charge my phone and reply back to you."

The beers were helping his hangover. Now he needed some aspirin, a pair of sunglasses, and something to eat. He also needed to find the bike he had borrowed and lost during the previous night's debauchery. The last place he remembered the bike was at Willie T's. He slid a twenty across the bar towards the newbie and said, "See you around."

It was six blocks down Duval to Willie T's. Between the little bar by the pier and the bar where he had met the woman, he knew he would be able to find everything he needed to help him survive the ill effects of an evening gone awry.

In his first couple of blocks, he stumbled into a CVS Pharmacy, where he bought aspirin and a big bottle of water. A few blocks up Duval, he stepped into a sunglass shop and found the same pair of Maui Jim aviators he had lost the night before. At the Conch Shack, he ordered a fried fish sandwich and another beer. By the time he got to Willie T's, he was starting to feel pretty good. He felt even better when he found the old bike miraculously still leaning against the brick and wrought-iron fence at the bar.

As he rode toward Trumbo Point, he noticed that the little island looked tired and worn. In the daylight, she looked like she had been abused and neglected for years. He noticed the faded paint on the buildings, the trash in the gutter, the overall broken-down look of everything that surrounded him. He had never noticed how tired Key West appeared, but then he wondered if perhaps it was simply him. He felt tired, broken-down, and neglected. He was growing old.

Arriving at Giles' home, he parked the bike where he had found it and headed towards his plane. Giles and another man were sitting by the pool. Orv groaned when he saw them. It wasn't that he didn't like the funny little Frenchman; he just didn't feel sociable after his rough night.

"Orville! It is so good to see you, my friend!" said Giles enthusiastically in his heavy French accent when he saw Orv approaching them. "I saw your plane yesterday and told my friend all about you. Come meet Enzo Pelletier; he is here again from Paris to enjoy our weather."

The man stood and offered his hand to Orv while Giles spoke to him in French. Then Giles turned to Orv and said, "Sit, sit, join us for champagne. I will open another bottle."

"Thank you, Giles," he said while accepting a seat under the umbrella at the table. "I had enough to drink last night. I will have a beer if you don't mind."

Giles took on a sympathetic look then laughed. "You look like the first night monster bit you last night." He scrambled towards the house, leaving Enzo and Orv alone at the table with no way to communicate with each other. Orv smiled, then leaned back in his chair. He pulled his hat down over his eyes and enjoyed the shade, wishing he had a cool bed to nap in.

The first night monster hadn't attacked Orv in more than twenty years, and while he would have openly denied that he had fallen victim to the monster, it was true. The monster was a fictional character that somebody had come up with long ago. It was the crazed animal that rode on tourists' backs during their first night of vacation, their first night of freedom.

Thousands of tourists a year over-drank on their first night in Key West, or whatever tropical location they had landed in. They blew off the steam they had accumulated over the previous year of sitting in some cubicle and dealing with the stresses of their day-to-day lives. In the islands, all that was gone. They drank, they danced, they had a ball. And it was then that the first night monster would attack, urging them to drink another shot of Wild Turkey at 3am. They let their hair down, drank more than they could possibly handle, slept with strangers—ball to the delight of the monster.

"Orville?"

He woke in the chair to the sound of Giles' voice. "Yeah?" he said as he sat up straight and adjusted his hat.

"You look tired," said Giles. "You should sleep. Take the beer and go to the guest room at the top of the stairs."

Orv didn't argue. He thanked his host, accepted the beer, and headed towards the house and the soft, cool bed that awaited him.

Giles yelled after him, "Please stay the night. We are going to have a nice dinner."

Orv waved over his shoulder as he moved away from them. He had a single focus: a bed and a pillow awaited him.

CHAPTER FOUR

Alice dressed in a casual blouse and a pair of khaki slacks for her day in the Keys. She wanted to look professional but not overbearing; friendly but not imposing.

She wasn't desperate to make a partnership with the local authorities in the Keys work. She didn't feel a sense of desperation to make her new operation work. But she had always been so driven towards success that she couldn't imagine it not succeeding. She couldn't imagine failure. She had become so accustomed to victory and to the pat on the back that came with it that she wouldn't know how to deal with anything else. She craved the positive attention from her superiors that came with a job well done, almost to the point of addiction. Success and praise were another desired high that came with her unhealthy need for overachievement.

Arriving at the office two hours before she was to meet Johnny, she dug up everything she could on the Monroe County Sheriff's Department and the Key West Police Department. She found nothing out of the ordinary with either; both seemed well-operated, efficient organizations. Both of their leaders had outstanding records and reputations. By the time Johnny Reno had arrived at the office, Alice had compiled a small dossier on each department and their leadership.

"We've got a lot to talk about," she said to Reno when he appeared at her office door. She scooped up the files and slid them into her briefcase, then said, "You drive. I'll bring you up to speed."

Traffic in Miami was predictably slow. As Johnny tried to find the quickest route south, Alice told him everything she had found about the two agencies, their histories, and their personnel. Traffic finally started easing up as they passed the zoo, but it didn't really clear until they were nearly to Homestead. They made good time for nearly twenty minutes before they hit the tourist traffic just south of Florida City. The two-lane Highway 1 from Florida City to Key West was almost always bumper to bumper with motorhomes and vacationers sporting license plates from around the U.S. Following the masses, they made their way onto Key Largo, across Tavernier, and finally to Plantation Key to arrive at the Monroe County Sheriff's Office.

"Remember," Alice said to Johnny as they walked toward the door. "We are polite, professional, and here to help."

Johnny laughed as he got out of the car. "The funniest line I've ever heard is, 'I'm from the government, I'm here to help.'"

Alice shook her head and shot him a glance as they walked towards the front door.

"Hi," said Alice with a big smile to the woman at the reception desk. "I'm Alice Weingarten. This is Johnny Reno. We have an appointment with Deputy Eubanks. We're a few minutes late."

They took a seat in the reception area and waited nearly ten minutes before a pleasant-looking, fifty-something uniformed woman appeared. "I'm Tana Eubanks," she said while shaking their hands and receiving their business cards. "Let's step into a conference room," she said before leading them through a door and down a hallway. Once seated in the rather blandly decorated room that held nothing more than a table, six chairs, and a flat screen TV on one wall, Eubanks said, "What can we do for the DEA today?"

Alice immediately picked up on tone she used. What she said was "today." What she meant was "this time."

Alice immediately turned on her charm. "It's not what you can do for us, the question is how can we help you." She saw a questioning look in the deputy's eyes and knew she had her attention. "As you know, the DEA in Southern Florida has long been focused on the mega-shipments of drugs coming into the area. We know there are still huge amounts of drugs coming ashore in the Keys by small boat and private aircraft. You fight this battle every day; you know the players, you know the territory. How can we assist you?"

The deputy's eyes narrowed with suspicion. She didn't hold back, she didn't try to be politically correct; she did what she had always been known to do. She spoke her mind. She displayed no anger; she simply stated the facts when she spoke. "I've been with this department for twenty-two years. Every five years or so, the DEA comes rolling into town to help us with our drug problem. You all come down here with your fancy shoes to help us country bumpkins stop the flow of drugs, something we're incapable of doing ourselves because you think we're better suited for writing parking tickets and manning school crossings. After six months or so, you guys get bored after using up our resources and go back north, leaving us with a thousand hours of overtime that we don't have budgeted and can't afford. You take credit for any little bust that does occur during your time here, but usually just mess up the investigations we do have in place. I don't mean to be rude, but go 'help' somebody else."

Alice sat quietly for a moment with a smile on her face before responding. "I know our history, and I apologize for my predecessors' actions. We don't intend to come down here and take over. We don't even plan to come down here, unless you ask for our help. What I would like from you is recommendations of your needs. What does your department need to stop the drug tide? How can we help you? Do you need money for overtime or more officers, use of our criminal labs, use of our surveillance aircraft and boats?" She took on a sympathetic look. "I know in the past we've acted badly, trying to take over down here. I promise you, this time is different. This time, we are here to help you. We're here to see what we can do to assist you with a very difficult task."

Deputy Eubanks stared at Alice for a long, contemplative moment before saying, "Excuse me for a second. I'd like to see if Sheriff Gothberg is available."

An hour later, as they walked back to their car, Johnny Reno turned to Alice with a smile. "Well, that couldn't have gone any better! You're in the wrong profession. You should be in sales."

They hadn't left Sheriff Cal Gothberg's office with anything set in stone, but they had gone a long way towards receiving forgiveness for the DEA's past sins. The two departments had agreed to work together, to share intelligence immediately and then to find ways to assist each other with a level of professional respect that had not previously existed. When the meeting with the sheriff was over, Deputy Tana Eubanks had walked them to the front door and then surprised Alice with a hug before they left.

Back in the car, Johnny turned back on Highway 1 towards Key West and looked at his watch. "I'll call Chief Brewer and see if he will be available for a late lunch. We won't get there until a little after one."

In her mind, Alice did the math. It would take them two hours to get from Plantation Key to Key West. Assuming they met with the police chief for an hour, they would be back in Miami just in time to catch the end of the afternoon rush hour.

She pushed the stresses and strains of living in a large metropolitan city away and tried to simply enjoy the ride. She hadn't been in the Keys for several years and had forgotten the beauty of the waters and the various mangroves. Passing on to Islamorada, she remembered driving down the islands with Orv, sometimes taking all day to drive to a friend's home on Big Pine Key. They would stop at any beach, gift shop, or other attraction that caught their attention. She loved those days. It was just the two of them, enjoying each other during the little time they had together.

As they passed the Catholic Church on the island, Alice remembered the amazing painting that hung in the church's narthex. "Have you ever stopped to see the painting at that church?" she asked Johnny. He nodded no. "If we have time on the way back, you've got to see it. It was painted by a local artist, a picture of Christ standing on the seashore. It's a still painting, but when you stare at it for a moment, it looks like the trees and the water and Christ's hair are moving with the wind. Absolutely amazing,"

Johnny shrugged his shoulders, saying nothing while concentrating on the road and traffic ahead. Alice caught glimpses of the man in the driver's seat. Johnny Reno was perhaps five years younger than herself. He was a good-looking man, not one a woman might notice right off in a room full of men, but a handsome man. As they drove across Indian Key Channel, she looked towards him. His profile, framed with the emerald blue island behind him, made him more than a casually good-looking man. At that moment, he was stunning.

While he was a married co-worker, a person she would never have romantic designs upon, she allowed herself a quick fantasy that she and Johnny were driving down to the Keys together. It was warm and comforting to have an attractive, strong man at the wheel. She lay her head back against the headrest, then Johnny turned and gave her a quick smile. For just a moment, her imagination ran wild. She shook her head and returned to reality. In her most business-like tone, she said, "Let me tell you what I know about Chief Brewer. We can compare notes and try to figure our best tactic for this meeting."

***

Orv was enjoying the mid-day alone at Giles' pool. He had napped for an hour then woke with the minimal effects of his hangover. Drinking some leftover coffee while sitting in the shade of a palm, he could see the Garrison Bight Mooring Field, an anchorage to at least a hundred sailboats that day. On some of the boats, which were at least a half a mile away, he could see people moving about, probably doing their daily chores or routine maintenance. He was reminded of something he had heard, probably something said by a fellow drunk in a bar or a line sung by a musician while he swilled another beer. "Life is filled with maintenance until the day you die. Don't let the details bog you down or life will pass you by." He thought about the words of wisdom. He had gotten so far behind and hadn't talked to so many friends and family members in so many years that he wondered if he could ever reconnect with them now.

After charging his phone, he found a text that read "DSU," indicating a landing at map code "D" on Sunday, which actually translated to Wednesday. Angel was already increasing the number of flights. He remembered without consulting the map that "D" indicated a rendezvous point at Lower Harbor Keys, out towards Jewfish Channel.

Giles had extended him an invitation to stay as long as he liked. Spending a free day on Key West made more sense than flying back up to Miami for just a day before his next flight to the Bahamas.

Giles' Land Rover was missing. He suspected that Giles and his guest were out on some adventure for the day. As the sun reached its mid-day position, Orv found the shade moving away from the pool deck and decided his pleasant morning was over. It had been so long since he had seen many of the sights around the island that he decided a bike ride over to Smather's Beach, down to Higgs Beach, and then past Fort Zachary before returning would be fun. It was a fairly long ride, considering that he hadn't ridden a bicycle for years. He would plan accordingly, stopping every now and then for food and drink. He was excited. It would be a fun afternoon.

***

The lunch with Police Chief Brewer started predictably. Even given Alice's past work with him, he was suspicious of the DEA's sudden interest in "helping local law enforcement" rather than ordering the locals around, as they had in the past.

"Do you know how many tourists come to the Keys each year?" he asked.

"About one point five million," Alice answered confidently.

Chief Brewer blinked his eyes for just a second, surprised she knew the answer. "Right. I have fifty-two uniformed officers to patrol twenty-four-seven. We have twenty-five thousand full-time residents and twenty-eight thousand tourists a week who come down here to warm up, cool down, or blow off steam. We have over three hundred establishments that serve alcohol on Key West. We host a major festival of some type nearly every week, from Fantasy Fest to Lobsterfest, the Mile Zero Fest, Meeting of the Minds, and dozens more. We've got airshows, boat races, parades, major concerts, fishing tournaments, and you want us to stop everything because there are some drugs being delivered to the islands? What do you guys do all day?"

Alice and Johnny both smiled thinly. "We're not asking you to stop anything," said Alice in a quiet and controlled tone. "We're here to see what we can do to help you. We have surveillance aircraft and boats, we have extra personnel, and we may have funds available to help pay your officers' overtime." She leaned forward and put her elbows on the table. "Would your job be easier if you didn't have five or six hundred pounds of narcotics crossing your shorelines every week?"

"Of course it would," said Brewer.

"Sheriff Gothberg thought so too; he's onboard," she said with a smile.

Chief Brewer stared at her for a moment, trying to determine if she was lying. He decided she wasn't. "If you got Cal onboard," he said with a bit of a chuckle, "we'll certainly help you in any way we can."

They left the meeting with a sense of cooperation that they had felt with the sheriff. They both felt that they might be able to really start to make a difference in stopping the flow of drugs into the Keys. In the car, they high-fived each other. It had been quite a day. Johnny started the car and backed out of his parking spot onto Catherine Street. He crossed Margaret and continued west.

"You know you're going the wrong way," said Alice. "Home is that way," she said while pointing her thumb over her shoulder.

"I haven't been down here since college," Johnny said. "If it's all right with you, I want to see Duval Street before we head back."

Alice shrugged her shoulders. An extra fifteen minutes wouldn't inconvenience her. She would likely spend a few hours at her desk when they returned to the office, despite the hour.

She looked out the window at the people on the sidewalks and in the shops, restaurants, and bars. They seemed to come from all walks of life. She noticed a homeless man with crazy hair having a conversation with an impeccably dressed elderly man in pressed white shorts and a golf shirt. It looked like the bum was giving advice to a millionaire. She saw people on scooters wearing oxygen cannulas and smoking cigarettes as they wheeled from bar to bar. Scantily dressed college-aged girls mixed with old men in tank tops. It was as wild an assortment of humans as she had seen since the last time she was here.

As Johnny turned onto Front Street, Alice suddenly started yelling, "Stop, stop the car!!!"

Johnny was being pushed by a delivery truck behind him while trying to get out of the way of a group of tourists crossing the street. "Just a second, I'll pull over right up there," he said as he maneuvered to a safe spot. "What is it?"

"Stop!" she yelled in a more frantic tone while looking over her right shoulder. He kept moving, looking for a safe place to stop the car. She threw open the door, causing him to slam on the brakes before she bolted from the car.

He pulled to the side of the road, blocking a parking lot entrance but at least getting somewhat out of traffic, then jumped out of the car and ran down the street after her. He didn't know what she had seen. He hoped she wasn't going after a drug dealer she had recognized on the street corner. He wasn't armed. The truth was, Special Agent Johnny Reno only carried a gun when he had to pass his annual certification. Other than that, his service revolver stayed locked in a gun safe in his closet at home.

He ran down the street in the direction Alice had gone and found her standing on the corner, wildly looking up and down the streets from the intersection. "What is it?" he asked as he ran to her.

Her face was flush with a desperate look in her eyes. Reno repeated himself. "What is it? Who did you see?"

She didn't know which direction to go, she didn't know where to run to find him. Johnny grabbed her by the arms, forcing her to look him in the eyes.

"Who did you see?" he asked the frantic woman once he had her attention.

"He was right here. I saw him," she said in a breathless voice.

"Who?" he asked again while holding her by the shoulders.

"My ex-husband."

***

Orv enjoyed his jaunt around the island. Returning back to Duval, he ducked into Sloppy Joe's for a cold beer but decided on a large iced tea instead. Enjoying the cool drink and the breeze coming from the ceiling fan, he thought over the decision he had to make: would he continue to fly for Angel? Between the five-thousand-dollar-a-flight raise and doubling the number of flights, after fuel and maintenance, he would clear about fifty thousand a week. If he logged eighty flights a year, he could contribute nearly two million dollars annually, assuming he didn't get caught.

A young woman played her guitar on stage. Her voice reminded him of Janice Joplin and he quickly decided he liked her style. He wasn't sure if the singer's name was Shasta or Tina or something like that. It was hard to hear what the young woman was saying over the loud Jersey woman at the next table who was telling her friend about a neighbor with a loud dog. Orv wondered which side of that fence was more obnoxious.

After the Jersey woman ruined a couple of songs, she and her friend paid their tab and left. Orv decided that the music was good, his stool was comfortable, and the breeze felt nice. He ordered a Cuban sandwich and settled in to enjoy all that was happening around him.

He used to often preach that "today is a gift." He told those who listened to live for today because tomorrow wasn't a guarantee, especially in his line of work. He needed to practice what he preached and decided that the afternoon would be just that. He would enjoy all the world had given him. He had an endless glass of tea, a big sandwich, and a pretty woman singing him songs under a cool ceiling fan. He didn't have much to complain about.

He realized he had been kidding himself about making any kind of decision regarding the future of his current employment while sitting in a bar. Over the past twenty years, he had made every major decision from the left seat of an airplane while flying at cruising altitude. He put off the decision to the following day when he would be flying to the Bahamas.

***

Agent Reno had a hundred questions as he led Alice back to the illegally parked, still running government sedan. "Are you sure it was him?" She only nodded in response. He was surprised by the emotions she displayed; in the year he had worked with her, she had been a rock-solid person, a leader who was all business. He had wondered at times if she had ice water rather than blood running through her veins. "We can drive around and look for him," he told her as they arrived back at the car.

Johnny turned back towards Duval, trying to keep his questions for later while searching for a bearded guy with a baseball cap and a bicycle, the thin description she had given him. Alice tried to compose herself.

"I'm sorry," she said after blowing her nose. "I didn't know that seeing Orv again would be so emotional."

"Did he see you?"

"I don't think so," she answered. She wiped her eyes before saying, "I haven't seen him in years, but he's been on my mind a lot lately for some reason."

"Does he live here?" asked Johnny.

"I don't know. We haven't talked since the divorce," she said while trying to see every person they passed on the street.

Johnny was in an awkward situation; he didn't know how much to pry, how deep to delve into her strange behavior. "You obviously want to see him. Why don't you give him a call?"

"I don't have his number. I don't even know where he lives," she answered.

Agent Reno stopped behind traffic at a light. Turning towards her, he said, "Are you kidding me? We work for the DEA; our job is to find people."

***

Orv woke feeling pretty good. He had enjoyed a decent night's sleep without the aid of alcohol, and neither of his demons had found him. He wondered if hiding in the Keys was the solution, a change of address, a change of venue. He had tried running from them before, but they would eventually find him and began their tortuous hauntings again. But that morning, he felt good. He was rested, sober, and able to enjoy a morning without a hangover.

Giles was up early as well and wouldn't let him leave without eating breakfast. After eggs and toast cooked by the little Frenchman, they hugged then walked together out onto the longboat dock where Giles helped him cast off.

He gave Giles a final wave as he turned to taxi towards the narrow strait between Fleming Key and the mooring field. As he made his way towards the strait, he radioed the Key West tower on 118.2 with his intentions. He hadn't planned a trip to the Bahamas before returning to Miami. He had only taken on enough fuel to get to the Keys and back. The only aviation fuel available on the island was at the airport. He would take off from the water, land at Key West International, and fill his tanks.

After receiving clearance for his short flight, he advanced the throttle and the prop. He looked over at the boats in the mooring field and felt a slight twinge of guilt, wondering how many of those poor souls were still sleeping as he shook them out of their bunks.

Once airborne, he turned west across Fleming Key into the northwest wind to gain altitude. Reaching a thousand feet, Key West routed him northeast for several minutes before turning him to the south for a few miles and then giving him vectors back to the west towards the field. He operated the lever that dropped the four little wheels down from the floats then wondered to himself the last time he had landed on pavement.

He quickly ran through a mental checklist in his head. Landing on pavement was easy; asphalt didn't move, it didn't have wakes from passing boats, it didn't have swells. A runway was a fenced-in controlled area without knucklehead weekend boaters, logs, or other hazards. He lined up on the centerline of Runway 27 and eased the Beaver down gently in the calm winds.

After turning off the runway, he taxied towards the transient parking area. In minutes, a fuel truck was beside him, and twenty minutes later, he restarted his engine. He had full tanks and had filed a flight plan from Key West to Marathon. Back in the air, he flew the airway south of Lois Key, then turned northeast towards Marathon at two thousand feet. A few miles east of the island, he radioed his intent to land at Boot Key Harbor. "Marathon Traffic, Beaver seventy-one whiskey tango final into Boot Key Harbor, water landing to the east."

He lowered his nose and took aim at the Boot Key causeway. Just before crossing the causeway, he looked down and to his left. He remembered that the Chiki Tiki Bar and Grille had a really good shrimp basket and he had always intended to get back there. Today wouldn't be the day. He reached towards his instrument panel and turned off his transponder, making him invisible to air traffic control.

After a low pass over the boats moored in the harbor, he climbed to five thousand feet and turned a few degrees to his right. He settled in for the one-hour-and-fifteen-minute flight to West Side National Park in the Bahamas.

***

Alice appeared at Johnny Reno's office door the morning after their trip to the Keys. She held two disposable coffee cups and had an embarrassed look on her face. "I'm so sorry for my actions yesterday," she said when he looked up. "I got you a coffee. Caramel macchiato, right?"

Johnny smiled. "You don't need to apologize, and you didn't need to get me a coffee. I get it, relationships are tough, emotions are tougher." He had been shocked at her reaction to seeing her ex-husband on the sidewalk. On the trip back to Miami, she talked non-stop about their marriage, the death of their daughter, his failed business venture in Jamaica, and their divorce. It was clear that she was still very much in love with the man. It seemed she had suppressed her feelings so deeply that when she saw him, they came busting out like a homesick angel.

"It was unprofessional of me. I acted like a love-struck school girl," she said as she handed him one of the cups.

Johnny took the cup, saying, "You acted like a woman who is still in love with the man she married. Can I help you find him?"

Alice physically took a step back. "I'm not in love with him anymore. I was just surprised to see him suddenly. It's been a lot of years."

Agent Reno knew better than to argue. "Do you have his full name and his date of birth? I'd be happy to see if I can find an address or a phone number for you."

"Thank you, but no," she replied. "That's against policy," she said as she reached into her pocket for a slip of paper. Dropping it on his desk, she turned and walked out, saying, "I would never ask you to do anything like that."

Reno smiled as he glanced at the paper on his desk, which contained a full name, date of birth, and a social security number for Orville Hendricks.

***

Forty-five minutes into his flight, Orv pounded his fist against the yoke and cussed at himself. As much as he had always said that it wasn't about the money, he knew these flights were all about the money. He would keep flying, he would keep earning the money, and he would keep sending the money as long as he could. He made a promise to himself to get out of the business the moment he suspected that the law was closing in on him, but he knew there was often no warning. One day, he would land somewhere and suddenly be surrounded by boats and helicopters, or he would be caught by the Coast Guard flying into the Keys.

If he didn't get caught by the authorities, numerous other career-ending scenarios crossed his mind. Someday he might be the body that washed ashore in Puerto Rico, or a man found in the wreckage of a plane that crashed and burned. He had recently heard of one contraband pilot who was the victim of a simple robbery. A rival group of showed up at a drop point and tried to take the goods and run. Nearly everybody died in the ensuing gun battle.

Survivors of this madness lived like royalty down in South Beach; those few who had flown saved their money and had gotten out. Orv had flown the flights, given away most of the money, and now didn't know how to get out.

Andros Island, The Bahamas appeared over the horizon, and fifteen minutes later, it took up most of his windshield. The Bahamians he met on the pickup side of his flight weren't as cautious as the others; they didn't employ a clever coded system like the one he used in the Keys. They always met him in the same place about the same time; the only factor that changed was the day of the week they met.

West Side National Park was a drug runner's haven. Spanning the entire west coast of the Andros Islands, its one and a half million acres of coastal mangroves, lakes and interweaving channels was protected by only ten park rangers. It was a perfect refuge for anybody looking to do something illegal without being found. Since the drug runners kept to themselves, had minimal effect on the wildlife, and left zero sign that they had been there, the park service placed their activities low on their priority list. The rangers were also keenly aware that the druggies were better financed than the park service. The drug runners had bigger weapons and faster boats than the rangers. It was safer to chase poachers, partiers, and litterbugs.

Crossing the mangrove coastline just south of Williams Island, Orv started a banking turn to the south into Pelican Lake. The skyline was clear of any aircraft. The only boat in sight was a white sport fisher he recognized. The man on the aft deck removed and waved his hat, signaling all was clear.

Orv set the flaps for landing, eased back on the throttle, and started scanning the water. The "lake," as it was called, was really a shallow inlet from the ocean. He always wondered why it hadn't been named Pelican Bay, which was much more accurate. The water was calm, the winds were light. He eased her onto the back of the floats and pulled the throttle to idle. As his speed bled off, he turned a hundred and eighty degrees back towards the approaching boat. He still saw only one boat in sight as he killed the engine and unbuckled his seatbelt.

Stepping down on to the float, he stretched as the boat neared. His .45 Ruger was under the seat but still within reach, an AR-15 was latched to the bulkhead behind the pilot's seat. These flights had become so routine that he had kind of forgotten they were there. As a precaution, he stood near the cockpit door until the boat swung around to back into his float. The captain's name was Alexandro, or that was what he told Orv a few years ago. His son was with him this trip. Orv couldn't remember the kid's name.

The kid handed twenty-six large gunny sacks to Orv, who threw them up into the cargo door, pausing once to crawl up and organize them. Alexandro took off his hat and nodded to Orv, "Two deliveries each week now," he said with a smile. Orv nodded, wondering how much they paid the skipper. He gave a wave to the two of them then crawled back up the little steps on the strut and into the cockpit where he began the startup procedure.

***

It didn't make sense. Johnny Reno had started the task with an almost cocky attitude. Give him a name, a date of birth, and a social security number, and in a few minutes, he could have anybody's home address, phone number, cell number, place of work, tax returns, bank accounts, credit report, and a copy of their driver's license. But in this instance, that wasn't the case. If he had to guess, he would have suspected that Orville Hendricks had died eight years earlier…except that he couldn't find a death certificate.

In the last eight years, Hendricks hadn't filed a tax return and no employment income had been reported to the IRS. His pilot's and driver's licenses had both expired and had not been renewed. He didn't appear to have a phone or a known address. He was either dead, working deep undercover for the government, or he had figured a way to fall so far off the grid that he left no electronic fingerprints.

"Alice," Johnny said as he stepped into her office. "Your ex-husband is off the grid."

"What do you mean?" she asked. She understood the term; she just didn't understand how.

"No taxes, no credit, no DMV, no FAA, no address or phone number," he said.

She looked at him with a questioning expression for a moment. "You're sure of that?"

"Yeah, it looks like eight years ago he vanished, maybe to another country, maybe undercover for legal or illegal reasons, but the guy is a ghost." He was careful not to offer the other possibility based on her reaction the day before.

Alice looked out the window for a moment before turning back to him. "I know that was him in Key West. He was wearing sunglasses, a hat, and a beard, but I know it was him." She shook her head, almost like she was shaking herself out of a trance. "Let's not waste any more time on my personal stuff. I'd like to set up an interagency meeting with the Coast Guard, the Navy, Monroe County, and Key West PD to start building a plan. Can you get that put together?"

"Yeah," said Johnny. "I'll see if I can get something on everybody's calendar in the next few weeks."

She frowned. "As soon as possible, please."

***

As forecasted, the winds had picked up considerably since his flight out. He would be bucking a headwind all the way back to the Keys. The winds and the turbulence buffeted the plane. Orv tightened his seatbelt then slipped into his shoulder harnesses before securing the aircraft's logbook, which was starting to float around the cockpit.

Thunderheads were building to his west again. He hoped he could either get in ahead of them or time his flight so that he could come in behind the storms. With a little over thirteen hundred pounds of ganja onboard and his fuel tanks two-thirds full, he was flying fairly heavy. The plane was rated to handle more weight but flying into a storm while heavy was never his preference. Planes simply flew better when they were light.

He watched the storm clouds as he approached the Keys with great interest. With the storm rising, he questioned his earlier decision to keep flying. This vagabond life was taking a toll on him. Bouncing around the islands in a tiny plane wasn't easy on a man his age. He noticed the older he got, the less he tolerated rough days, like the day this was quickly becoming.

His flight path took him along the southern shore of Marathon Key and followed Highway 1 down the Seven

Mile Bridge. At Bahia Honda Key, he turned northwest to try to skirt around the big thunderheads that hung over Cudjoe Basin. He hoped to get north of the storm and come in behind a squall line moving across Snipe Keys. In his years of flying this route, he had never once had to divert due to weather, he hoped this wouldn't be the first. There was no contingency plan if he couldn't land or if the boat wasn't there. He was sure that Angel would be a little upset if he dumped a half a million dollars of dope into the sea, but it wasn't his duty to babysit the cargo, only to deliver it.

North of Barracuda, he caught a break. The skies behind the squalls were clear. Turning back to the southwest he would follow the islands for about fifteen miles until he came to Jewfish Basin and Lower Harbor Keys. He hoped the weather hadn't scared the newbie bartender/boat captain into staying at the dock.

Just as he started his descent, two Navy F-5N Tiger-2s appeared through the clouds in front of him, about a thousand feet higher. The single-seat fighters were likely out on a routine mission, but Orv knew that the Navy was always on the lookout for suspicious aircraft or boats. Finding a seaplane sneaking around the clouds in bad weather might pique their interest. He leveled the plane and watched them as they passed overhead. Once they were above and behind him, he had no idea if they were turning to follow him or not. Turning left or right would give him a view towards the back, but if they were following, that would look very suspicious.

He turned south and continued his descent then started looking for the boat, which he hoped was there.

***

The phone call from Key West Police Chief Brewer came as a surprise to Alice. She had given him her card and asked him to reach out to her at any time, but she hadn't expected him to call the next day.

"I was up half the night thinking of initiatives we could put in place if you were serious about working together," he told her.

She smiled. "I've been given a lot of latitude on this assignment. You tell me what you need to stop the flow onto the Keys and I'll figure out how to get it to you."

"We know the guy who's bringing the drugs in, a Puerto Rican National by the name of Angel Moritz. He comes and goes as he pleases. He even passed through customs. Hell, we know he was here last week. But everything we have on him is circumstantial. If we could infiltrate his communication system, we might be able to take apart his organization."

Alice wrote down the name, Angel Moritz. "I'll see what we have on this guy and check with our people in Puerto Rico. If we can get close to him, we might be able to capture his cell number. Then we'd be able to hear every phone call and see every text he sends or receives."

There was a discernible pause on the other end of the line. "You guys can do that?"

"Yes, that technology has been around for a few years," she replied. "The next time you find out that your guy is in town, you let me know, and I'll fly a guy down there to see if we can get his cell signal."

Brewer chuckled. "How close do you have to get to him?"

"Our equipment can identify cellular signals within a twenty- to thirty-foot area, then we start weeding out the ones we know are not the suspects. We often find these guys in airports or restaurants, so there may be fifty to a hundred cell phones in that small of an area. But we've had good luck finding our perp's signal."

"What other Buck Rogers's technology are you guys hoarding over there?" asked the Chief.

"There is one other thing you might be interested in," she said. "The FBI and TSA have been working with a software company to build a program that enters radar transcripts into a big database. They then can look for aircraft that come and go on a regular basis from uncontrolled landing strips, small airports, or in your case, water. The program searches for planes that leave from the Keys and fly out of radar contact towards Cuba, for instance, then return from the same direction. Those aircraft identified as suspicious could then be further investigated."

"Wow," said Brewer. "What about boats?"

"Boats under a certain size aren't required to identify themselves with the AIS system. But in theory, the database might still be of some use. It can identify patterns, a craft that runs between Cuba and the Keys every Tuesday, for instance."

Alice paused for a moment then said, "Hey, while I have you on the phone. I thought I saw a guy I used to know when we were there. Do you happen to know a guy named Orv Hendricks?"

Chief Brewer thought about it for a moment before replying, "No, I don't believe I do."

"No problem," she said. "It might not have been him. If it was, he might have been there on vacation. I thought it was worth a try."

***

The appearance of the Navy Tigers wasn't a coincidence. An aircraft was observed on radar approaching Key West without squawking a transponder signal. The fighters, already on the tarmac for a training flight, were directed to seek and identify the craft. Their take-off was delayed by weather, but they found the Beaver shortly after takeoff. They identified it as a non-threat, recorded the tail number, and went about their planned flight.

***

Orv spotted the tired old red Springer sport fishing boat in the channel off Lower Harbor Key, right where he expected it. As he made his approach, he saw the man on the flying bridge remove his hat, signaling an all-clear. The waters in the strait were still rough from the passing storms, almost too rough to land, but he spotted an area that looked a little calmer than the rest. He was in no mood to spend any time circling to see if conditions got better. He set the floats down on the water and received a jarring bump as the plane went airborne again and twisted to the right. He gave her a touch of throttle and a little left rudder and set her down again. This time, she stayed on the water.

As he taxied towards the approaching boat, he watched the water and shook his head. It was rougher than it looked coming in under the gray light of the cloud-obscured sun. When the boat neared, he shut down the engine. Jack backed the boat towards the plane as Orv climbed down onto the float. The wind and the water made everything difficult. The boat wanted to swing into the wing; the plane and the boat both pitched in the swells. They finally got a rope tied from a rear port cleat to the strut of the plane so they could start tossing weed.

"Rough son of a bitch today," said Jack with a smile as he grabbed the first bag.

"Yep," replied Orv in a tone that he hoped said "I don't want to talk, I just want to unload and get out of here,"

"How many bags do you have today?" asked Jack.

Orv handed over another bag. The guy was probably a really nice person. In a different time and place, Orv might have enjoyed chatting with him over a beer. But this wasn't the time or the place to make friends, or the place to waste time on idle chit-chat. "Twenty-six, I think," using the same, irritable tone.

"Wow," replied Jack with a laugh. "That's quite a load!"

Orv smiled and shook his head. The kid just wasn't going to get it.

***

As Orv bounced his way north towards Miami, Alice sat at her desk mired in deep thought. Had that been Orv on the street corner? Why had he fallen off the grid? If it hadn't been him on the corner, had he moved to some little village in a foreign country where he lived off what he could make fishing? Had he died in an unreported accident?

She opened the file Johnny had given her. All of his debts had been paid more than eight years earlier. His credit cards were still open, but the account balances were zero. His social security number hadn't been used, the IRS had not recorded income from W2's, tax returns, or investment accounts over the years. His driver's license, passport, and general aviation pilot's licenses had all expired. There were no cars, boats, or airplanes registered in his name in the U.S.

She stared out the window, remembering that Orv had never seemed to deal with Jessica's death. With the failed airline in Jamaica, the loss of his partner in New York on 9/11, and the resulting legal problems, losing his license to fly, his daughter's struggles with life and eventual death, and his crumbling marriage, he had so much to deal with and she hadn't been any help to him. She sat in a deep stupor in their darkened bedroom for weeks. When she finally got the strength to resume her life, he was too far gone. When she did see him, he was either drunk or hungover. Most of the time, he simply didn't come home.

Alice realized that afternoon in Key West that she wanted to find him. She wanted to talk to him, to let him know that she didn't hate him. She didn't blame him for any of the horrible things that happened so many years ago. She wanted to apologize for her behavior, for not being there to support her half of their marriage, for being a bad partner when everything was crumbling around them. She admitted to herself that she still loved him very much.

Closing the file on her desk would feel like she was abandoning him again. She knew it was silly, but she pushed the open file folder to the right side of her desk and went to work on other tasks.

***

Orv arrived back at his apartment just after eight in the evening. He was beaten and tired from a long day of being bounced by storms. On his way home, he had stopped by a convenience store for a twelve pack of beer and a frozen burrito. He drank two beers while his burrito heated in the microwave and then set the box of beer next to his chair in the living room. While watching some mindless sitcom, he ate and drank and hoped sleep would come easy. By eleven, the beer was gone and he had fallen asleep in the recliner.

Alice came to him in his dreams, but it was a different dream than in the past. She was warm and gentle. They played on the beach; they teased each other and laughed. They hugged and kissed and walked hand in hand along the water.

Orv woke and looked around the apartment for her but quickly realized that she wasn't there. He sat up and thought about her, wondering what she was doing, where she was, if she had remarried. The dream had been so different from his dreams of the past. She wasn't angry, he wasn't hurt, they weren't sad. They were two people in love with each other. He wondered if the woman in the sedan he saw passing him on the street corner in Key West had really been her. It had been so many years and it was only a glance, but the woman in the car had certainly reminded him of his beautiful Alice.

He sat awake in his chair and tried to remember the past. He wanted to remember the good times. There had been so many. They had been so in love, but he seemed to have suppressed those memories and had only remembered the hurt and the pain for so many years. He needed to remember the good and to push the painful memories away. He knew the past got hazy with time, but he also knew that if he looked, he would find a big ol' stack of happy yesterdays in the corner of his mind.

In the light cast off by the TV, he looked around the living room of his little apartment. He could stow his entire life in a duffle bag. He looked down at himself. His clothes would make good rags. In all the years that had passed, he hadn't accumulated much at all. He hadn't done much that anybody could point to when he was gone to say, "Orv did that," or "Orv made that." When he was gone, he would leave behind no legacy. He likely wouldn't even have a headstone at a cemetery. When he was gone, he'd simply be forgotten, dust in the wind, as the old Kansas song said. He had no family and no real friends. He was on the road to a sad and tragic end.

He thought back to his dream of Alice. Smiling, he faded back to sleep, but in his happy slumber, Yellow Eyes came to visit him again. The cruel little man mocked him and spit on him before taunting him with his weapon. It was the same nightmare all over again.

CHAPTER FIVE

Arriving to work on Monday morning, Alice got a cup of coffee then listened to the only voicemail that had come in over the weekend. "Good morning, Agent Weingarten. This is Deputy Eubanks with the Monroe County Sheriff's Department. I may have a lead. Give me a call when you are available."

Alice picked up the phone and dialed the number. Eubanks answered quickly. "Thanks for calling me back," said the deputy. "I have a possible lead for you to chase. I looked into it, but it seemed to run into a dead end."

"Great," said Alice. "How can we help?"

"Friday afternoon, the Navy tracked a small plane approaching the Keys from the east, not transmitting a transponder signal. Private aircraft are not required to use a transponder, except when operating in controlled airspace, but the Navy and Coast Guard has been trying to watch for them because these days, it's just suspicious. They had a training flight put eyes on the plane. It was a float plane. The pilots thought it was a de Havilland Beaver with a tail number of N71WT. When I looked up that registration number, it came up as a Cessna 210 registered to a company in Kemp, Texas. I called the company out there in Texas. They said their plane was in a hangar at the local airport and that it has never had floats on it."

"Interesting," replied Alice.

Eubanks continued, "Then I called the Kaufman County Sheriff's Department and asked them to check it out. They called back and verified that a Cessna 210 with that registration number, and wheels, was indeed in a hangar at the Harbor Point Airport."

Alice looked up at the ceiling for a moment before responding. "So either the Navy pilots didn't read the tail number correctly or we have a small float plane flying around the Keys with no transponder signal and a forged registration number."

"Yes, Ma'am," said Eubanks, happy that she didn't need to spell it out for the DEA agent.

"I'll look into it and report back to you, Deputy Eubanks. Is there anything else I can do for you?"

"No, Ma'am," responded the deputy.

"Why don't you call me Alice?" she said.

"Only if you will call me Tana."

Alice smiled. "It's a deal. I'll get back to you, Tana."

Alice looked at the tail number she had written on her pad, N71WT. She wondered how close the pilots had actually gotten to the plane and if they had misread or jumbled the numbers. A number seven could look like a one or an "L," and the "T" could be mistaken for an "I." There could be a hundred possible combinations, one which might belong to a float plane owned by a law-abiding citizen. Or her original thought might be correct. Somebody was playing games with their registration numbers.

***

Orv woke from a fitful night's sleep. He checked his phone and was happy to see there were no new text messages and no missed calls. He cracked open a beer to take the edge off his hangover and thought about his day. He needed to spend some time working on his plane. It needed to be cleaned out. He could probably sweep up enough spilled marijuana to supply a small college party. And he wanted to do some general maintenance. Every month, he religiously went over her carefully to tighten screws and bolts, check cables for wear, grease fittings, and look for anything that might need a mechanic's attention. It was a habit he got into in the service. The mechanics in his unit were top notch, but he was the guy up in the sky. He was the guy who hoped they hadn't missed anything.

He planned on spending most of the day working on his plane, but first, he decided to return to his chair to nurse his hangover and try to remember and enjoy the dream about Alice. In the past, he had been haunted by the pain, the frustration, and the anger associated with all that had torn them apart. The previous night's dream had been much different. She had that smile that he had fallen in love with in high school. She looked at him with those irresistible eyes, they laughed, and they loved again.

As he remembered the dream, he also remembered the good times, the amazing love, their early years that were so good. He wasn't sure which was harder, waking after a night of pain and anger or last night's visions that made him miss her so much.

***

"Alice Weingarten," she said after picking up her ringing desk phone.

"Good morning, Agent Weingarten. This is Don Brewer in Key West. We've just been notified that Angel Moritz cleared customs at Miami International. I don't know what good that information does you, but I told you I'd call the next time we had a hit from them."

"What time did he clear customs?" she asked excitedly while imagining a movie scene of police swarming the airport and SWAT teams rappelling into the terminal on ropes.

"About a half hour ago," said Brewer.

A half hour, she thought to herself. He would already be out of the airport by now. She was about to tell the police chief, politely, that the information was a little too little and a little too late when she had another thought. "Customs would know what flight he came in on, right?"

"Yes, I have that information. They said he came in on American Airlines flight 472 out of San Juan, Puerto Rico."

She quickly wrote down the information on her notepad. "We'll never find him in Miami, but you may have just given us the information we need to start unraveling Mister Moritz."

"Really?" he asked with a tone of intrigue.

"Yes," she said with a lift in her voice. "If he flew into the States using his own passport, he's already shown us either he isn't too smart or he's cocky as hell. He likely paid for his ticket with a credit card. The airline can provide us with his credit card information, and from there, we can start unwinding his finances. He probably uses that card for all of his travel, so if he buys tickets in the future, we'll be ahead of him rather than behind him. We'll know where he's going to be and when. And, he likely pays that credit card from his primary checking or savings account. That account could be a treasure trove of information."

"That's fantastic. Can you get a search warrant to cover all the accounts?" asked Brewer.

"We don't need a warrant," she said with a smile on her face and in her voice. "After 9/11, Congress gave us the Patriot Act. The act doesn't distinguish between drugs or terror; it gives us sweeping authority to investigate all enemies of the United States, foreign and domestic."

Chief Brewer breathed an audible sigh. "We get so caught up down here dealing with drunk tourists and locals selling joints that we probably aren't even aware of all the tools available to us." He paused for a moment, "I'm pretty excited to be working with you and the DEA, this time."

Alice grinned. "We're excited to work with you too. Between us, I think we can do some real damage to their infrastructure and maybe even go after some of the leaders."

She promised to get back to him after they spoke with the airlines.

***

It was going to be a warm day in Miami. The temperature inside the plane was already sweltering as he climbed aboard with a small broom. After sweeping up the dirt and dust and the remnants of his last several cargos, he deposited the plastic bag full of debris into a garbage can then started his monthly maintenance routine. Two hours later, he went into the little bathroom at the seaplane port and tried his best to clean the dirt and grease from his hands. His shirt was soaked with sweat, his face dripped perspiration.

Walking back to button up the plane, he remembered the old Adirondack chair that sat in the shade of a palm on the left side of the ramp. He decided to sit for a while and let the breezes cool him before completing his tasks for the day. It was one of his favorite spots. From the chair, he could see the comings and goings in the harbor. He could watch boats and ships of all types pass; it was an endless show. He gazed at the activity before him and thought about her and about their past. They had such great dreams and so much hope for their future. He remembered her saying, "Hope keeps your dreams afloat" whenever he was down. If that was true, he was the owner of a sunken boat. His past was sad, his hopes were shot.

His phone rang just as he started to mentally sink into a dark place. "Yeah?"

"Are you in Miami?" asked the familiar voice.

"Yes," Orv replied.

"There's a bar in Little Haiti, Churchill's Pub on 55th. Be there at two o'clock today."

Orv shook his head. He was getting tired of Angel ordering him to these meetings on short notice, as if he were an employee. But the man paid him huge sums of money, and the work was easy, if not risky. "Two o'clock, Churchill's Pub," Orv repeated before snapping his flip phone shut.

He had never met with Angel in Miami. They usually met somewhere in the Keys. He had met with him once in Puerto Rico and a few times in the Bahamas. He wondered what the meeting was about but was also happy that they were meeting in a public place. Sometimes Orv worried that Angel might choose to replace him with a younger, less expensive pilot. He didn't imagine that his termination meeting would be in a public place.

After checking his watch, he rested his head against the back of the chair and spent the next half hour watching the activity in the channel. He could have taken a nap, but he resisted. Two people from his past were always there, always lurking, always waiting to invade his dreams.

***

Alice didn't know who to contact at American Airlines and the bank that administered Angel's Visa account, but Skip Bowman certainly did. Skip had been recruited to the DEA from his desk job at the Secret Service, where he mainly investigated counterfeit transactions.

Years earlier, the serious big money criminals had quit counterfeiting currency and started dealing in interbank transactions. They had figured out how to forge wire transfers to request large transfers from one bank to another. The Secret Service, who has been the guardian of America's currency since its inception, got involved.

An hour after Alice gave Skip the information, he walked into her office holding a couple of pieces of paper and the hint of a grin. "This guy's not the brightest bulb on the string."

"What do you have?" Alice asked with a smile.

"He bought his tickets with a credit card issued by Chase Bank. I'll have a couple of years of his credit card transactions before the end of the day," he said while trying not to sound too proud of himself. "His credit card is paid off every month by a transfer from Banco Popular de Puerto Rico, an FDIC insured bank based in San Juan. Transcripts of his last two years of transactions with them will probably be on my fax machine when I get back to my desk."

"What could he have done to make your job more difficult?" she asked out of curiosity.

Skip laughed and shook his head. "Well, first of all, if you're breaking laws in the U.S., don't use banks that we federally insure and monitor. It will be interesting to see if he has multiple credit cards and multiple bank accounts or if he is really that dumb."

"Good job. Let me know what you find," she said. Alice knew she worked with some of the best investigators in the world. She had a talented team and tried to tell them how much she appreciated them every chance she got. It wasn't natural to her to offer a simple "good job" to one of her team members, but she was trying to remember to compliment somebody every day on their work. Her team made that task easy.

Her own investigation of Angel Moritz turned up a plethora of information. He was born in February of 1967 to a single mother. He got caught committing his first crime when he was eleven, petty larceny. From twelve to eighteen, he was in and out of the juvenile system. His last crime was an auto theft a few days after his twentieth birthday, then he seemed to either figure out how to stay straight or how to avoid being caught for years.

In the late eighties, a DEA report associated him with the Martinez family, who was known as the Puerto Rican cartel. The family, headed by the notorious Quitoni Martinez, grossed an estimated $750 million a year from international drug deals, extortion, and loan sharking. Their activities had grown and started expanding into Mexico, and soon they started having problems with the Gulf Cartel, which eventually grew into a full-scale war. The war raged on both Puerto Rican and Mexican soil, resulting in numerous kidnappings and murders. At some point, Angel slipped away and filled the void created by the murder of the drug boss of the Florida Keys.

While he had been identified as a person of interest in Southern Florida by the DEA, their investigations hadn't reached that far, until now.

Alice was excited to learn more about Angel Moritz and to figure out if he was just a logistics man or the head of the snake. Once they uncovered his role, they should be able to figure out where the drugs came from, who was supplying them, and who was moving them to the U.S.

***

Orv arrived at Churchill's Pub a few minutes early but purposely waited in his car until he was a few minutes late. He parked on NE 2nd next to a bright red double decker London-style bus that sat in a vacant lot across the street from the pub. The bus might have served as a restaurant or bar at some point, but now it was an obnoxious, graffiti-covered billboard.

The bar had been there for several years. It was an English pub located in a rough and rundown central Miami neighborhood. Walking in, Orv let his eyes adjust for a moment before looking around for Angel and his ever-present sidekick thug. He found them sitting at a back table. Angel smiled when he saw Orv.

"We've certainly been seeing a lot of each other lately," said Orv with a wink. "People may start to talk."

Angel laughed. Orv thought he heard the thug growl. "Please have a seat," said Angel with a chuckle.

"What can I do for you?" asked Orv.

"I've identified a new…issue," answered Angel. "With the increased sales coming from the north, we have increased cashflow."

"That doesn't sound like a problem," said Orv.

Angel smiled and looked towards the ceiling, purposely trying to make a point that the pilot didn't understand the business. "Too much cash is my biggest problem. The cash from my sales around the Lower Keys was easily laundered or used to fund other investments in Florida. But we've already had great success in the Upper Keys and even on the mainland. I anticipate even more sales, and more cash. I'm going to ask you to start flying cash to the Bahamas when you make your regular flights."

Angel was right, Orv didn't understand the business and had no interest in understanding anything beyond his little part in it. He was a pilot flying cargo. That was the most he wanted to know. In his mind, Angel was paying him to fly from Florida to the Bahamas and back. It didn't matter to him if he flew out empty or full; it was Angel's flight.

"Okay," he said without emotion. "Where do I pick it up?"

"Is it safe to meet you at your airplane on the morning of your flights?" asked Angel.

Orv was surprised that Angel asked for his advice. "No, I don't need any of your shady cohorts lurking around my plane with bags of cash," he replied while glancing towards the muscle, who returned an intimidating stare. "I'd rather meet somewhere public to pick it up. A grocery store parking lot, Costco, Winn-Dixie, somewhere with lots of cars coming and going."

"That would work just fine," said Angel. "My associate will contact you by phone to set the first pickup. You will be flying again tomorrow, so watch for a text."

Orv gave Angel a nod then stood. He turned to his thug, who stood a few feet away, and they glared at each other for a few seconds before Orv laughed, shook his head, turned, and walked towards the door.

The text message indicating the next day's flight came before he got back to his apartment. He parked, responded to the text with a single character, "Y," indicating "yes," then started towards his second-floor apartment.

Before reaching the top of the stairs, his phone rang. "Yeah."

"Hey, how about we meet at the Winn-Dixie on 11th Street, off the expressway and I-95 at 8:00am tomorrow morning. Would that be okay?" said the man on the other end of the line. The voice surprised him. In his experience, the people who ran the organization were short and to the point. They spoke abruptly on the phone, almost always portraying an attitude of hostility. This voice was different. It sounded like he had been called by a California surfer/stoner.

"That works," said Orv. "Don't be late."

"No problem," said the voice. "See you in the morning, dude."

Orv looked at his phone. Did the guy just call him "dude"?

He stepped into his apartment, locked the door, turned on the TV, and settled into his easy chair. After searching through the channels, he found nothing on worth watching, so he settled on a *Hogan's Heroes* rerun he had seen a number of times. If nothing else, it was noise, something to help fill the lonely void of a dismal, nearly bare apartment. He looked around and noticed that his apartment was much like his life, pretty gloomy and depressing. Something needed to change.

The first apartment that he and Alice had lived in had been very similar to this one. They had probably been built in the same era. Alice had fixed the place up, all on a tight budget, but when she was finished, it had felt like a home. He tried to remember what she had done to make the little space look so warm and comforting. Flowery drapes, a few plastic plants, a fake flower arrangement on the table, a lamp here, an end table there. Orv imagined this apartment fixed up, but realized no matter what he did, it would still be depressing. What had made that apartment feel like home was Alice.

***

By the end of the day, Skip Bowman had already compiled an impressive collection of bank statements and credit card information on Angel Moritz. He promised Alice he would dig through it at home, after he had dinner and helped his wife get their kids to bed. He was excited to see what he could find in the pile of faxed information. "This is usually just the beginning," he told her. "Bank and credit card statements are like the trunk of a tree. If we follow them, they begin to branch off and eventually lead to more and more branches. At the end of each branch is an interesting leaf."

Alice smiled at the excitement on his face and in his voice. She remembered that feeling. She missed that feeling and wanted to feel it again. She was excited to take down Angel Moritz and all of his associates.

While she had only been at the Agency for a few years, it had already come to feel like just a job to her. She had become an administrator, a valuable team leader, according to her annual review, but another bureaucrat in a sea of bureaucrats. She longed for that feeling of danger. It had been far too long since she had worn a bulletproof vest and held her 9mm pistol while crouched behind a shrub row waiting for the "go" signal.

Even though she had promised the local law enforcement that the DEA was just there to help out, she decided that she wanted to wiggle her way to the frontline when they took down Moritz and his group. She and her agency could hang back in the shadows during the press conferences, they could give all the credit to the Police and Sheriff's departments, but she needed to be there for the takedown.

***

Orv woke in his chair. He was surprised that he had fallen asleep. The light flowing through the window indicated it was early evening. He rubbed his eyes then looked around the room. It was still the same depressing little apartment. He stood and walked to the window then pulled opened the drapes. Even the view was depressing. Beyond the empty, abandoned swimming pool was a parking lot full of old, beat-up cars. Across the busy street was a sea of old, broken down buildings. It was no wonder that he was depressed; everything he saw was gloomy and disheartening. He needed a change in his life. He needed something in his life to be bright and fresh and new. He longed for something to get his blood flowing again.

A new and exciting relationship was his first thought, but then he remembered the last several women he had pursued. They had each ended badly, leaving him feeling even worse than before. Hell, he thought to himself, even the whores couldn't be trusted. In a weak moment a few years earlier, he had hired an escort to add some excitement to his life. She had agreed, at an exorbitant fee, to act as his girlfriend for a few days. He woke the first morning to find that she had not only taken her fee for the three days and ran, she took his wallet and a stack of cash he had hidden in his closet. His one marriage had ended badly. He had taken too many gambles in that crazy foreign land, but poor performance and lack of attendance finally did him in.

Women weren't the answer, he told himself again. Perhaps he needed to change his life completely. A new country, a new profession, a new Orv. Maybe he could be a bartender at one of the funky little joints near Marigot Bay on St. Lucia. He wondered how much it paid.

Orv remembered the incredible Marigot Bay. It was a tiny anchorage on the western shore of the island of St Lucia, a place he and Alice had once visited when he was flying cargo around the Caribbean. It was the kind of place that he could imagine Ernest Hemmingway hanging around, although he never heard of Papa being there. It was an anchorage that should have appeared in one of Hemmingway's novels. If a movie were ever made, his main character could have been played by Humphrey Bogart. He had often thought Marigot Bay would be a great place to hide out if he ever needed to disappear. It had been years since he had last been there. He hoped that it hadn't been discovered, that it was still as beautiful as it had always been.

His stomach growled, his feet itched, he needed to get out, he needed to move. Orv realized how much he had enjoyed his time in Key West. It was fun to be around people. He hadn't really understood until now just how solitary his life had become. He rarely spoke with anybody. He flew his flights then spent the rest of his time sitting around his apartment with the blinds pulled, waiting for his phone to ping. His life needed to change.

***

Alice arrived at her office earlier than usual the next morning. She was surprised to find a report from Skip Bowman already on her desk. Instead of opening the report, she picked up the phone, dialed his extension, and asked him to come to her office.

When Skip arrived, he asked, "Was there anything wrong with the report?" Alice had heard that type of response before; her predecessor had been somewhat of a tyrant. The man had expected his subordinates to read his mind, to give him information he hadn't requested. When she took over the division, she inherited a group of brow-beaten professionals who were good at what they did.

"I haven't even opened it," replied Alice. "I thought I might get more out of it if we went through it together."

A look of relief washed over Skip's face. "I'd be happy to show you what I found," he said with a smile as he sat down in one of the chairs at her desk.

Angel Moritz might have been really good at moving drugs onto the Keys, but he wasn't very good at covering his tracks. His Chase Visa account and the checking account at the Puerto Rican FDIC insured bank were both open books. The Visa showed where he had traveled, where he had dined, and where he had slept for the last year. Skip assured Alice that he could access previous years if needed. He also pointed out that Angel never seemed to travel alone. In almost all cases, he had purchased two airline tickets and reserved two hotel rooms.

The Visa bill was paid in full each month by the same checking account. The Banco Popular de Puerto Rico checking account showed a few other interesting items, regular money transfers to two people each month. An amount of $5,000 was paid the first of the month to Camila Moritz. Skip did a quick search and found a sixty-eight-year-old woman by that name, which Skip explained was probably Angel's mother. He was still working to confirm that. The other monthly transfer was to Ezequiel Soto.

"I searched for Ezequiel Soto," said Skip. "The guy's an interesting character. He was born the same year as Angel and in the same town, a sketchy suburb just south of San Juan. The guy has a rap sheet full of minor crimes that's longer than my arm. Most of his crimes are assault and battery, tampering with evidence, obstruction of justice, and every parole violation you can imagine. About four years ago, he suddenly turned clean. He either found a good Catholic woman to set him straight or he found a job that required him to stay out of trouble. My guess is that this guy is the bodyguard that travels with Angel."

He went on to show Alice that the checking account received regular transfers of differing amounts from a bank in the Cayman Islands. In the last twelve months, the transfers from the Caymans to the Puerto Rican bank had totaled just over sixteen million dollars. The current balance in the checking account was two hundred and ninety-seven thousand dollars.

Skip looked up from the report. "Getting information out of the Cayman Islands is still difficult, but no longer impossible. I am working to get my hands on that account."

Alice smiled. "That's really solid work for less than twenty-four hours. Good job!"

Skip returned a sheepish, "Thanks." He told her that he would update her immediately if he found anything else of consequence, otherwise, he would let her know when his report was complete.

Alice knew the people that worked on her team were top notch, some of the best. They just needed to hear some positive affirmations from their supervisor to really make them shine.

After getting a cup of coffee, she sat at her desk and tried to sort through all of the information that sat scattered before her. Angel Moritz was starting to become a real, three-dimensional person right before her eyes. He was the starting point to tearing the whole network in the Lower Keys apart, and he seemed to be making it reasonably easy for them. She had the description of a suspicious floatplane and the ability to track Angel's movements.

But she remembered that he was only one person. A thousand boats a day that came and went from the islands, any one of which might be bringing in the drugs. She also reviewed a recently received memo from the National Parks Service that said they suspected that drugs might be passing through Dry Tortugas National Park and Fort Jefferson.

The memo went on to say that hundreds of tourists a day visited the island via private and charter boats and charter float planes. Alice thought about it for a moment. To smuggle more than a few pounds of drugs a day would be difficult unless the employees of the charter companies were involved. A few pounds of pot would be nothing, but a few pounds of cocaine would be a significant amount of smuggled contraband. She added the charter employees to her growing list of suspects.

***

Orv was up. He checked the weather along his route and groaned. It would be another bumpy day but not nearly bad enough to cancel the flight. He left in plenty of time to make it to the Winn-Dixie in time, actually arriving early enough to do a little shopping beforehand. After purchasing some granola bars, bananas, and a few bottles of water for his flight, he returned to his car then looked around the parking lot for a person looking to get rid of a big stack of cash. He had no description and no meeting point. He simply was looking for somebody who appeared to be looking for him.

He spotted John right away. Orv shook his head and rolled his eyes as he hopped into his car and drove to the southwest corner of the parking lot. He had never actually met John, but he knew him by reputation and had seen him around the islands for years. Orv didn't think that John had any business being involved in the profession. He was a naive pawn in Angel's dangerous game.

John, as he was known down island, had been born Charles John Imes. He had grown up in a disjointed family. His father left when he was young, his mother worked two jobs to make ends meet. His grade school and junior high years, however, had left him with incredible memories, growing up with his next-door neighbor and best friend, Jack. Together, with his imagination and the tales from the books that Jack loved to read, they had amazing adventures. High in the magnolia tree, they shot down enemy fighter planes. They won the pennant, pretending to be Micky Mantle while hitting rocks in a field by the road, and they played Napoleon Solo, living the life of a spy.

In junior high, Charlie started to rebel against the heavy-handed nuns at St. Teresa's Catholic School. He was kicked out and forced to attend public school after getting into a fist fight with Sister Irene. It wasn't a fair resolution;

97

he always contended that she started the fight. At different schools, Jack and Charlie drifted apart. Jack's life turned to academics and sports while Charlie became interested in cars and girls. They remained friends, but the tight bond slowly slipped away. After high school, Jack went off to college, Charlie went to fight the war.

Charlie's time in Vietnam was cut short when he was injured in an ambush during his third month in country. Cut down by a machine gun while walking up a hill, he distinguished himself by tossing grenades up the hill at the gunner who was cutting down his squad. His last, lucky, on target toss earned him the silver star along with a purple heart and a medical discharge. Charlie threw both the medals away.

Orv knew him as John, a name Charlie had taken when he arrived down island. He was an eclectic character, a strange bird. John had long unkempt hair and a beard that seemingly could hide all sorts of items. He always wore a crushed straw cowboy hat, which earned him the nickname "The Old Beach Cowboy." John rented rafts from a little shack on Smather's Beach when the weather was good and when he felt like showing up. Along with his raft rentals, he had sold pot by the joint to the tourist on the beach. Orv had often seen him either at the beach or riding his bike around the islands, usually with a beer in a koozie he had taped to the handlebars.

Normally, Orv would have met the drop man, taken the bag, and left without a word. In this case, he didn't feel like he could walk away in good conscience without saying something to John.

In a court of law, John wouldn't have been able to truthfully answer that he had ever seen Orv before this moment. By design, Orv had tried his best to be a figure hiding, just a shadow, a face easily forgotten when he disappeared. "Looking for something from Angel?" asked John.

"Yeah," answered Orv. As John turned to his old pickup, Orv said, "It's none of my business, John. But you're in way over your head here."

John turned, surprised that the pickup man knew his name and seemed to have an opinion about him. "Do I know you, man?"

"I've seen you around the islands," answered Orv. In his years since the war, Orv had become good at spotting a fellow vet. John was completely contrary to a typical military man, but Orv could still tell, somehow, that John had been there. He also knew that he hadn't returned from Vietnam as a whole person. The scars on his legs below his shorts could have come from anything, but John had scars that weren't visible, not to the normal person. To a fellow vet, somebody who had done time in country, somebody who had lain in a military hospital bed, somebody who still lived the war at night, John's previous service was easily recognizable. Orv felt a compassion and a need to help if he could.

"I'm in over my head?" John asked. "How do you know what I'm into?"

Orv looked at the ground for a moment. "It's none of my business. I'm afraid that Angel is jumping over some dangerous fences up here and you're the one that he's putting at risk."

John smiled while handing over a green duffle bag to Orv. "Nobody seems to care that we're selling up here. I can take care of myself."

"Every ounce you sell north of Matacumbe takes money out of somebody's pocket," Orv said while taking the bag from John. "Somebody cares," he said as he hoisted the weight of the bag of cash in his right arm, "and somebody is eventually going to tell you about it."

"Maybe," said John quietly.

Orv could tell he wasn't going to convince the man of anything. He was probably overstepping his bounds and he might even face retaliation from Angel if John told him about this exchange. He started to turn to leave then said, "You need to be damn careful."

John nodded and smiled then turned back towards his truck.

After tossing the bag in the trunk of his rusty Camry, Orv watched John drive off, a thin cloud of blue smoke trailing from the old pickup. Orv shook his head and hoped the guy understood the trouble he was getting himself into.

He drove across the causeway and into the Seaplane Base parking lot. With his flight bag over one shoulder and the duffle bag over the other, he walked through the empty office and out to the ramp where he saw his plane sitting on the ramp. He loved the old bird. She looked like he did: tired and worn. Her faded paint, her dents and dings made her look like her owner just didn't care too much about her, but it was all just window dressing, just a facade.

Since Orv spent about ninety percent of his time flying over water, and forty percent of the time hauling marijuana, he maintained Seventy-One Whiskey Tango impeccably. General aviation aircraft require regular maintenance performed by a certified A&P mechanic based on the number of hours flown. Orv threw that schedule out the window; it was far too lenient for his liking. He kept the guys at Boca Aircraft Maintenance at the Boca Raton field busy. Gary Weaver, one of the head mechanics at the facility, loved the old plane and loved working on her big nine-cylinder Pratt and Whitney radial engine. Every time Orv taxied up to the hangar at Boca, all the mechanics would drop what they were doing on the fancy jets they maintained and come out to see the plane.

"Fueled, full, and ready to go," said Scotty when he saw Orv emerge from the building. "Let me know when you're ready and I'll help you push her in."

"Thanks," he replied as he walked to the plane. After securing the duffle bag and doing a quick walk around, Orv climbed up on the float and then into the cockpit and tossed his flight bag on the seat next to his. He turned on the master power switch and pulled up his course on the GPS.

When he was ready, he climbed back down to the float and then down onto the ground. Scotty helped him pull the wheel chocks and then give her a push over a small lip at the top of the ramp. Gravity did the rest. Orv followed the plane down while waving over his shoulder then leapt onto the back of the float.

Most pilots wouldn't let their plane drift out into a busy harbor without the engine running. If it didn't start, they would have to signal the base for help and wait for them to send out their little skiff to pull them back. Orv never had a problem starting his baby. She hadn't let him down in years. Before he had drifted twenty yards off the ramp, he had her fired up and pointed downwind towards the line of white cruise ships.

Five minutes later, after receiving clearance from Miami Center, he checked the gauges. The oil temperature was in range, the manifold pressure looked good. He radioed his intentions to any other aircraft in the channel area then turned into the wind and advanced the throttles.

As he lifted off the water, a crosswind blew him uncomfortably, but not dangerously close to a Royal Caribbean ship moored off his left side. He could see passengers hanging on the rail watching his takeoff and let her drift a little closer before he banked away from the ship. He shook his head at his little stunt. He always wanted to be an invisible man, yet he was naturally a bit of a showman. He turned south and started following the ATC directions to get out of Miami airspace.

CHAPTER SIX

As Orv was flying out of the Miami area, a morning meeting was taking place at a closed trendy bar in Pompano Beach. Typically, these meetings were held once every two to three months, but this one had been called as a special meeting to discuss a new and growing threat to the organization. The goal was to create a plan to mitigate the new threat without creating any additional problems for the group.

"Thank you all for coming in so early," said Tom Eason while raising his coffee cup to his four associates sitting at the bar, acknowledging that none of them were early risers. Their business largely took place after sunset. If they saw sunrise, it happened just before they went to bed. "As you know, Angel Moritz started dealing north of Matacumbe several weeks ago. Now I'm told he has moved on to the mainland and has been selling in Miami."

The three men and one woman sitting before him each shook their heads and frowned but said nothing. "I reached out to him and asked him to meet with me the other day, but he didn't show up," said Eason with a look of concern. "Out of respect and civility, and before we do anything drastic, I'd like to try to at speak with him at least once."

In the six years since Tom Eason had taken over, the Greater Miami area had enjoyed a relatively cooperative and peaceful drug distribution system. Eason's rise to power came when his predecessor was killed in an earlier turf war. With nobody in the organization to fill the void, Eason, the accountant, had stepped forward to run the Miami cartel.

His first act had been to partner with several of the surrounding area leaders, even factions that had been involved in previous battles. He talked them all into coming together under a common umbrella, managed by himself. Within a few years, he was in charge of all of the cocaine and marijuana distribution south of Lake Okeechobee, drawing a line from Jupiter on the east coast to Charlotte Harbor on the west. The only distributor he hadn't been able to convince to join him was the little Puerto Rican in Key West. Eason dismissed the Lower Keys. While it was a profitable area, he had plenty to manage in his own territory.

Running the Southern Florida distribution system like a business, without emotion or greed, Eason had grown it to a nearly billion-dollar-a-year enterprise. Threats to the business from outsiders were nearly nonexistent. With virtually no violence in years, Eason had commanded respect from his associates and his peers. Even local law enforcement respected his organization. The local media hadn't reported on bloody bodies on the streets in years, like during the drug wars of the past. Eason's organization operated with quiet efficiency and very few people were interested in upsetting that apple cart.

Looking over his small but loyal team, Eason asked for their opinions to this new threat, asking his most trusted advisors what he should do about the little Puerto Rican.

Dennis King spoke up first. "We've made it very clear, over the last five or six years, that you don't deal south of the lake or north of Matacumbe. Everybody knows that, Angel knows that. The time for talk has passed. I say we send a direct message to him." Everybody looked at King. They all recognized the problem; they were hoping for a solution. "I've heard the guy he has dealing up here looks like a homeless bum, and he drives a beat-up old pickup," he continued. "We can rough him up and send him back to Angel with our message. Or his pilot flies out of

Watson Island. We can take out our frustrations on him and his plane."

Eason winced. "We might get there, but let's not start with violence. How do we get Angel's attention?"

"The pilot's not a bad idea," said Gil Wiseman. "If we disrupt his supply line, we'll get his attention."

Eason tilted his head slightly to the side. "Okay, there's two ways to go about that. The risky way is to beat the guy to the point he can't fly for a while, or we screw up his plane so it has to spend a few weeks in the shop. The safer move is to leak to the cops or DEA that the guy is flying drugs."

Every head in the room turned towards Becky Denton. The petite, pretty redhead looked back at the four men staring at her. "What?" she asked in a slightly irritated voice. Becky was the closest thing to a double agent that existed in the organization. She worked for the *Miami Herald* as a metro beat reporter with strong alliances to local law enforcement and she moonlighted as an informant and confidant to Eason and his organization. Several times, she had alerted the cartel to changes in police procedures or policies that had saved the organization from being disrupted by busts.

"Yes, I can tip off the right people and get the plane searched and probably seized," she said. "That's actually why I wanted to attend this meeting. There's a convenient change in the wind."

"What's that?" asked Eason.

"There was a big meeting at the DEA last week," Becky said with a smile. "It comes from the top. They want to shut down the small distribution channels. They have a whole section dedicated to taking down the boats and planes delivering small loads to the Keys."

"Which group?" asked Wiseman.

"Alice Weingarten's group," she answered with a grin.

Eason smiled. Never in the history of organized crime had a criminal organization known so much about the law enforcement community that pursued them. Becky Denton was an easy recruit; she was an adrenaline junkie who thrived on action and reveled in knowing the inside scoop on any organization. She loved to be "in the know." He'd met her on a flight from Atlanta to Miami and liked her instantly. By the end of the flight, they exchanged business cards, hers from the *Herald*. His simply said, "Tom Eason, Consultant."

A few days after they met, she reached out to him. She wanted to know more about what he did. She told him that her inquisitive side wouldn't let her stop thinking about their conversation. Eason knew better than to tell a newspaper reporter anything about his business, but she knew a lot about it already. "I did a little poking around," she told him over the phone. "You went to work for the accounting firm, Arthur Anderson, after college. Then I found that you quit that job and went to work for a company called Fishhead Imports. You've worked there, making a small annual income for ten years, even after the owner, John Carvelli, was murdered in South Beach."

Eason remembered being suspicious, asking her, "Why are you digging into my past?" Her answer surprised him.

"I have an unquenchable thirst for knowledge and want to know how things work. I want to learn more about your business, the inner dealings, the structure, the logistics," she said. "If you help me understand, I can help you understand the structure of those who pursue you." It was clear that she knew who he was and what he did. They met for lunch, and before he paid the tab, she had convinced him to hire her.

As a group, they spoke through the pros and cons of leaking the pilot and airplane to the DEA. Deciding that might be a better option than roughing up the pilot, they chose that method. Becky would drive to the seaport after the meeting and discreetly get a photo of the plane. She would chat with the employees there to see if she could get the pilot's name, then give the information to a local snitch she knew who would in turn sell it to the DEA for a few bucks. When they confiscated the plane and arrested the pilot, Eason would reach out again to Angel, admitting that the pilot's arrest was his doing and asking the little Puerto Rican if he was ready to talk.

After the meeting, Becky Denton drove to the seaport under the guise of researching and writing an article on seaplanes and their economic impact on Southern Florida. When she arrived, there was no airplane matching the description she had been given. The employees had no interest in giving her any information. When she took the direct approach and asked about the old seaplane, the Beaver that used to sit over in the corner, they said they hadn't seen that plane in years.

***

A stiff tailwind made Orv's flight out to the Bahamas shorter than usual, but he took no pleasure in the time savings knowing that he would soon be flying back into that same wind.

Thoughts of Alice, little strings of memories, played in his mind as he flew. He hadn't spent much time thinking about her during the days. She usually only occupied his nights. But the woman in the car a few days earlier had brought her back into his conscious mind. He enjoyed the pleasant memories; his mind was filled with the times she laughed and smiled. He missed her.

Orv checked his watch as he began his approach to the inlet. He was early, and he didn't like to spend a lot of time on the ground. The tailwind was whipping up whitecaps on the water, but they were small, easy to handle. He flew to the south of his landing zone, looking for the white fishing boat or any other boats in the area. Seeing none, he banked the plane sharply around, pointing the nose into the wind as he lined up on the water below. The winds were blowing fifteen to twenty he guessed as he set the flaps and leveled his wings. He eased back on the yoke and let the tails of his floats test the water. The plane gave a playful little hop then settled into the water and quickly slowed.

As the Beaver settled, Orv turned her a hundred and eighty degrees to the east to look for the boat. It appeared that he was alone in the area. He shut down the engine then climbed down onto the float to pee. Checking his watch again, he saw that he was at least fifteen minutes early. He had been early before, but the boat had always beaten him to the lake. An uncomfortable feeling came over him. He considered beaching the plane on the sandbar to his south but instead decided to drift east with the wind for a bit and hope that the familiar white fishing boat appeared quickly.

He didn't have a lot of options if the bad guys showed up while he sat on the water. It wouldn't take him more than a minute to crawl back in the cockpit and start the plane, but getting the plane up to speed to take off took a lot of time. If the bad guys—he used the term to describe both law enforcement and actual bad guys, competitors or thieves—had a plane or helicopter, they would be on him before he could get away.

As the plane drifted, so did his mind. He had a big bag of cash to deliver. He wondered how much was in the bag and if that had any bearing on the boat not being early. Having never been in this predicament before, he wondered how long after the appointed meet time he should wait before he took off and returned to Miami. As a number of scenarios, all bad, raced around in his head, he saw a motion to his east. The white sport fishing boat was rounding the point and heading towards him. He breathed a sigh of relief but refused to let his guard down. He reached under the seat and retrieved the .45 Ruger he kept stashed. He tucked it into the small of his back, into the waistband of his shorts under his Hawaiian shirt.

A hundred yards away, he saw the man at the helm remove his hat and wave to him. He recognized the old fisherman and waved back, and a comforting feeling came over him. A few minutes later, he loaded twenty-nine bags of pot aboard, more than he had ever taken. He handed the old man the duffle full of cash, and the man lifted it and said, "Business is good!" Orv just smiled in acknowledgement, shut the cargo door, and headed for the cockpit. It was going to be a bumpy ride to the Keys, he thought again as he looked out at the winds.

He felt his phone vibrate in his pocket as the engine roared back to life. Fishing it out, he saw he had received a text from Scotty at the Seaplane Base. The text only had two characters, "TU." Orv cussed then tucked the phone under his thigh as he advanced the throttle. "Tango Uniform" was the message. "Tits Up" was the translation. The Seaplane Base had been compromised.

Orv eased the plane off the water and climbed to a thousand feet before starting a banking turn to his westerly course. He didn't know what to expect when he got to the Keys. He didn't know what he was flying towards. If some faction of the law had been looking for him at Scotty's place, which was what the coded message indicted, a swarm of DEA boats, planes, and helicopters could be waiting for him at Barracuda Keys. The unpleasant thought of spending the rest of his life in prison crossed his mind.

It was almost the same distance from the Bahamas to the Keys as it was to Isabela de Sagua, a beautiful little peninsula on Cuba's north coast. Once there, he could either toss his shipment into the Bahia de Carahatas or try to sell it to the locals. With the money he made from the sale of his plane and Angel's drugs, he could live comfortably for many years in a little shack by the sea. It sounded much more pleasant than a little prison cell.

***

Undeterred, Becky Denton went back to her office at the *Herald* and started searching websites. Not knowing what a Beaver looked like, she searched for a picture of one, quickly found it, and printed it. The Seaplane Base website had a couple of photos of seaplanes, but none of them looked like the photo on her desk. Several of the aircraft on the website were owned by Miami Seaplanes, a tour operator. Searching their website, she saw the obligatory photos of their aircraft, in the air or beached on a beautiful sandbar. Just as she was about to close their webpage, she saw a photo of one of their planes on a beach. She spotted another aircraft in the background of a photo. Leaning forward, she could see an older plane, obscured and blurred in the background of the photo. Comparing what she could see to the photo she had printed, it looked like a Beaver. Zooming in on it, she could just make out the numbers on the fuselage, N71WT.

It was a bit of a stretch; she wasn't sure she had found the right plane. She didn't completely believe the guys she spoke with at the base. Becky had noticed a glance between the two young workers in the office when she mentioned the plane. She decided to call her contact at the DEA. Mark Young answered his cell phone after four or five rings. "Hello?"

"Hi, Mark, it's Becky Denton. Do you have a moment?"

Mark had known Becky for a few years. She had provided him with some good tips in the past. At times, she would call for additional information on a story she was working, but sometimes she had information obtained through her sources. The young, energetic reporter had built a tight underground information network. She seemed to know everything that was going on around town. "Sure! What's up?"

"I've got a source that said that there's a seaplane here that's been delivering drugs to the Keys on a regular basis. Interested?"

Mark shook his head. It was as if Becky knew they were targeting planes and boats in the Keys. "Of course I'm interested. What do you have?"

"I don't have much," said Denton. "I've been told there is a de Havilland Beaver that is often at Watson Island, at the Miami Seaplane Base. He gave me the registration number, N71WT. My source said the plane flies a couple of times a week out of Miami, goes somewhere south, and delivers a bunch of weed to the Keys."

"The plane is based here?" Young asked.

"Yeah," she said with half a chuckle. "Right under our noses."

"I'll check it out," said Young. "Same deal as always?" he asked.

"Yep, when you take them down, I want the story."

***

Alice sat at her desk sifting through piles of information. Often, the clues were there, in the data, a little piece of information here, a snippet there, an arrest, an accident, or a familiar name. Someday, all of the information from the DEA, the FBI, the Pigeon Forge

Police Department, and every other law enforcement agency would be fed into a computer. When a name was typed in, all of the information about that name would appear with little arrows linking it all together. But for now, very few of the systems were linked and there were no little arrows pointing out relationships and coincidences. It was all still done by hard-working investigators.

Johnny Reno passed by her door then stopped and turned around. "Did you get the calendar invite I sent you?" he asked. "The interagency meeting is set up for next Thursday in Key West."

"Great!" she said with a smile. She was surprised at how quickly he got it put together, considering all the calendars he had to coordinate. "Do we have room for the whole team?" she asked.

"Yeah, I booked the large conference room and some smaller breakout rooms at the Fairfield Inn."

"Excellent! Let's supply lunch as a goodwill gesture. I'll see if I can book the Beechcraft to fly us down, so we don't spend ten hours on the road that day."

Johnny smiled. "Sounds good. I'll arrange lunch," he said before he continued down the hall.

Mark Young stepped into her office and waited for her to look up. After a moment, he cleared his throat, causing her to look up. "Hey, Mark, what's up?"

"I got a lead on an old seaplane that has been making drug runs into the Keys,"

Alice smiled while quickly sifting through the pile of paper before her. "An Otter? No, a Beaver," she said as she found her notepad. "Tail number N71WT?"

Mark looked down at the sticky in his hand. "Yeah," he said in a slightly surprised voice. At the same time, he was shocked that she already had the information yet not surprised that she had it before him. He had learned that she was an amazing investigator.

"Have you run the tail number through the FAA?" she asked. "It comes back as a Cessna in Hull, Texas. The sheriff down there confirmed the plane was a Cessna on wheels. What do you have?"

"My source said the plane is often sitting at the Miami Seaplane Base on Watson Island, off the MacArthur Causeway."

"That's what, forty-five minutes from here?" she asked.

"About that. Wanna go for a drive?"

She smiled. A field trip would be much more pleasurable than spending the rest of the afternoon with her piles of paper. "Let's go!"

***

Orv didn't know what to do or where to go. He didn't know what the message from Scotty had really meant, or how serious it was. It could have been as minor as a police car turning around in the parking lot or it could mean there were DEA agents swarming the base. It was hard to make decisions based on a two-letter code they decided on years earlier that meant "Dude, don't come back here."

He needed more information, but he couldn't call Scotty from the plane while in the air. He would never be able to hear him. If the entire operation had been compromised, landing out at Barracuda Key could be his last landing ever. If the message was a simple warning, flying to Cuba, his alternate, with a plane full of dope might be the wrong reaction. He decided to land at Mud Key Channel, a few miles southwest of Barracuda Key. From there, he could call Scotty and decide if he was going to risk the rendezvous at Barracuda or turn south and try to make it to Cuba. He cussed the headwind that was sapping his fuel.

It was nearly the same distance from Barracuda to Miami as it was to Havana. If the winds kept up, he might have to risk refueling at Key West to get to either destination. Landing in Cuba without a visa was a crime punishable by imprisonment. Landing at the remote Isabela de Sagua, he would have to hope the officials would accept a bribe to waive the normal documents. He could try telling them he had misread his compass and flown the wrong way, like his childhood hero, Douglas Corrigan.

While most kids became inspired to fly by heroes like Charles Lindbergh and Amelia Earhart or fighter aces like Eddie Rickenbacker or Pappy Boyington, Orv had always been intrigued by Douglas Corrigan. In the nineteen thirties, Corrigan decided he wanted to follow Lindbergh and fly solo across the Atlantic Ocean, from New York to Ireland rather than to Paris. He knew quite a bit about the flight; as an airplane mechanic, he had worked for Ryan Aeronautical in San Diego and helped build Charles Lindbergh's *Spirit of St. Louis.*

Unlike other aviators at the time, he didn't have Howard Hughes' money or Lindbergh's sponsors. He only had a dream. In 1933, he purchased a used 1929 Curtis Robin monoplane for $310 and began to modify it for his transatlantic flight. He built a more powerful engine and installed multiple fuel tanks. The Bureau of Air Commerce refused to certify his airplane for a transatlantic flight, deeming the aircraft unsound for such a journey. After years of modifications and battling with bureaucrats, he was finally issued a certification for a transcontinental flight in 1938.

On July 9th, 1938, Corrigan left California for Bennett Field in Brooklyn, New York. One of the fuel tanks he installed inside the plane developed a leak during the flight. Corrigan had to hang his head out the window to keep from becoming sick from the fumes as gallons of gasoline sloshed around his feet. He arrived in New York with just three gallons of fuel left in his tanks.

On July 17th, he departed Bennett Field for his return flight to California with 320 gallons of fuel, a quart of water, a couple of chocolate bars, and two boxes of fig bars. He took off to the east in cloudy weather. After takeoff, Corrigan should have turned to the west and flown to California, but twenty-eight hours later, he landed at Baldonnel Aerodrome in County Dublin, Ireland. He bounded from the plane saying to the shocked field manager, "I'm just in from New York. Can you tell me where I am?"

Orv loved the story of the pilot who claimed, until his death, to have accidentally flown the wrong direction. The press nicknamed him Wrong Way Corrigan. His flight captured the imagination of people weary from the Great Depression and worried over news of an impending war. When he arrived back in New York, Mayor LaGuardia threw him a ticker tape parade that was attended by more people than had gathered for Lindbergh's parade. He had thumbed his nose at authority and achieved his dream, and that gained Corrigan a permanent place in Orv's heart.

Of course, any smart official in Cuba would look at Orv's plane, with two compasses and GPS, and immediately question his story of flying the wrong direction. He hoped cash would solve the problem. Looking at the GPS, Orv noticed a slight uptick in his groundspeed numbers; the headwinds were lightening a bit. The turbulence was not.

***

Arriving at the Seaplane Base, Alice and Mark Young first tried to peer into the fenced-in area to see if they could identify a Beaver with the correct tail number. Only four planes were visible. It looked as if other planes were there, just not viewable from their vantage point.

"Let take the direct approach," said Alice.

Mark looked at her with a slight frown. "You're not worried about tipping them off?"

"We don't have enough information to warrant a stakeout if the Beaver isn't here," she answered. "Let's go ask them about it. Maybe they don't know they have a drug plane based here."

Mark shrugged his shoulders. She was the boss. They walked back to the car and drove to the Base office. Entering the office, they were greeted with a cool blast of air conditioning and the smell of grease and fuel that filtered in from the adjoining hangar area.

"Good afternoon," said a man from behind a cluttered desk behind the counter. "How can I help you?"

"I'm Agent Weingarten with the DEA, this is Agent Young. We had a couple of questions; do you have a moment?" Alice always liked to ask people if they had a moment to chat. If they answered yes, they had just committed in their minds to be cooperative and to give her some of their time.

"Sure," said the man as he rose from his chair. "I'm Scotty Steadman, the Base manager. How can I help you?"

"We're looking for a particular plane, a de Havilland Beaver," replied Alice.

Scotty acted surprised. "That's a pretty rare plane around Florida. Finding it shouldn't be hard."

Opening his small notebook, Agent Young said, "This one is orange and white. The tail number is N71WT."

"I know that plane," said Steadman. "It's been through here a time or two. You'd never forget an old Beaver like that."

"We understand it's based here," said Alice.

Scotty gave a surprised look. "No, the only planes based here are the tour planes. The only private seaplane here is that Seamax M-22 out there. It's owned by a doctor here in town."

Alice looked for anything in the man's face that would indicate he was lying but determined he was either telling the truth or he was a hell of a poker player. "Do you know the pilot's name of the Beaver?"

"Probably," he said as he moved to a computer on the counter. "We've ramped and fueled him several times over the years. I haven't seen him in months, maybe a year, but let's see if I can find the last time he was here. We should have his credit card info on file. Give me that tail number again."

Alice gave a smiling glance at Mark Young. The base manager could ask them for a warrant, but he didn't seem concerned about releasing the information. A name and a credit card number would be an incredible amount of information.

"Here it is," said Scotty. "N71WT, a Beaver. He was here on April 7th. We ramped him for two days and fueled him. He paid six hundred and forty-three dollars, cash. He was here a few months before that, one day and fuel, he paid cash. Last year, he was here for two days. He paid cash. We didn't take a name, just the tail number."

"Is that normal?" asked Young. "To not get a pilot's name when they come through here?"

"Yeah," said Scotty. "We're a filling station. It's like when you buy gas for your car. If you pay cash, they don't care what your name is."

"How many of your clients pay with cash?" asked Alice.

"It's not the norm," replied Scotty. "It used to happen all the time, but we've become such a plastic society that it's rare; not unheard of, but rare."

Alice was still looking for the telltale signs of a liar but wasn't sure she saw anything in the man. "And you're sure the Beaver hasn't been here since April?"

"No, Ma'am," he replied quickly. "I'm not here all the time. But I can tell you that if he's been here, he hasn't paid for any services since April. We are diligent about entering every transaction: cash, credit, or chickens."

Mark and Alice looked at each other. They both knew there was nothing else to learn here at the moment. They thanked the base manager. Alice left her card and asked him to call her if the plane arrived at the base in the future.

As Scotty watched them pull out of the parking lot, he sent a second text to Orv. "TU X 2."

***

Orv fished his cell phone out of his pocket and read the new text as he started his approach into Mud Key. He wondered what it meant. He hadn't responded to the first message, Scotty must have wanted to make sure he got it and that he wasn't coming back to the Seaplane Base. He tried to type a message one-handed while flying the plane with the other, but with the turbulence, he decided it was impossible. He would be on the water in a few minutes.

A single boat, a thirty-foot pleasure craft, sat anchored in the strait where he typically landed. It wasn't unusual to see a boat like that out here. He banked to his left and lined up on the western side of the Key. The leeward side was his preferred choice, simply because of the calmer waters, but the swells weren't bad. He timed them, setting the plane down just over the top of one, purposely bouncing over the next, and then took the third on the nose of the floats, which slowed him quickly while spraying a flume of water over his windshield.

As his speed bled off, Orv turned the Beaver ninety degrees to the left while looking for boats or other aircraft. Confident that he was alone, he turned her back into the wind, shut off the engine, kicked open the door, then climbed down onto the float. To his left were the mangroves of Mud Key, to his right another tiny island. Before him was water as far as he could see. A small squall was passing to the south of him, but the clouds to his west seemed to be breaking up. The only sounds were the wind and the water lapping against the floats.

After sending a text to Scotty—"Can u talk?"—Orv leaned against the side of the plane and tried to imagine what would cause his friend to send two texts. It may have been that he didn't reply to the first. The bigger question was, what had caused Scotty enough concern that he sent the first?

His phone rang. It was Scotty's number. "Hey," said Orv. "What's up?"

"We've had a busy day here," said Scotty. "This morning, some woman stopped by asking about your plane. The guys told her they hadn't seen the plane in a few years. A few minutes ago, I had two DEA Agents in the office asking about the plane. I told them I knew the plane but not the pilot, and I hadn't seen the plane for several months."

"Did they buy your story?" asked Orv as he kicked the strut of the plane.

"I think so," replied Scotty.

Orv looked out across the water for a moment. He had always known what he needed to do in this scenario. There were no other options. "Well shit, Scotty. I hope I haven't put you in a bad way. Thanks for all you've done for me. It's been a pleasure."

"Send me a postcard from Alaska or the Yukon Territory someday," said Scotty. "Let me know if the fish up there are really as big as they say."

Orv smiled. They had never talked about this day or his plans if it ever came. Perhaps Scotty's reference to Alaska was a hint of where he thought Orv should go, or maybe it was where he might lead the DEA to believe he went. "Are we square financially?" asked Orv.

"We're more than square," answered Scotty. "I appreciate the business and the friendship. You be careful."

"Thanks, man," said Orv before he pressed the end button. He was going to miss Scotty. Maybe someday they would bump into each other and do some fishing together, but it seemed unlikely.

With that, he turned the phone over and removed the battery. Then he tossed it into the brackish water of the channel. A few minutes later, after he tossed the last bag of Columbia's finest into the water, he climbed out of the back of plane and stood on the float as he watched twenty-nine bags float away and slowly sink.

CHAPTER SEVEN

"Did you believe him?" Agent Young asked Alice as they drove west across the MacArthur Causeway.

"I think so," she answered with a slightly pained look on her face. "But I found it strange that he didn't seem to think that somebody paying him thousands in cash for fuel and services over time was suspicious, which I question."

Mark glanced over at her. "I want to believe him, but something just doesn't smell right."

She smiled. It was that kind of intuition that made good investigators. "Go with your gut," she said. "What can we do to follow up?"

Mark looked out at the water to his left as he thought. What could they do to check the manager's story? "Satellite imagery," he said after a minute. "I'll look at satellite sweeps of the area and see if I can spot the Beaver sitting at the base sometime in the recent past. Airplanes spend at least ninety-five percent of their lives on the ground. That one has sat somewhere."

"Great idea," said Alice with a smile. She was sure she wouldn't have thought of it.

***

Orv climbed back up to the pilot's seat and turned on the GPS. He punched in the letters "IDS" and the coordinates for Isabela de Sagua came up on the screen. The calculated distance was 160.89 nautical miles. He cussed under his breath while checking the fuel gauges. The gauges on the old plane weren't horribly accurate.

There was no way to tell exactly how many pounds of fuel he had on board.

He did his calculations based on his best guess of what fuel he had left, what his burn rate was, the distance to the tiny village, and his guess on the winds aloft. He figured he had enough to make it there, assuming the winds remained generally on his tail. If the winds died down, if he had to fly around any large storm cells, or if he couldn't land immediately due to a passing squall or some other reason, he wouldn't have any reserve.

Under any other circumstances, he would never fly across the Florida Strait without more than enough fuel to get there and back, but he couldn't risk landing at Key West to refuel. His options were limited, and he was making a mistake that killed many aviators: he was allowing outside factors to make reasonable pilot decisions.

With that thought in mind, he hit the starter button and brought the old bird back to life.

***

Immediately after Alice arrived back at her office, Skip Bowman came in with a file folder and an excited look on his face. "What have you found?" Alice asked.

Skip looked like a guy who had just discovered the cure for cancer. "Cayman bank records used to be nearly impossible to obtain and almost as hard to decipher. Since 9/11, the Caymans have become much more accommodating. We know Angel receives huge deposits from an account in the Caymans. I'm still trying to figure that out. I've also found that he pays a set amount on a fairly regular basis to another Cayman account. It's been twenty-five thousand dollars almost every week for years. I think those might be payments to his delivery man."

Alice smiled while she thought through the scenario he presented. Why else would a drug distributor transfer a set amount of money on a regular basis to an offshore account? "That seems plausible," she said. "Who owns that account?"

"Here's where it gets tricky," said Skip as he opened the file. "The funds go into an account at Butterfield Bank, but the account is owned by a Limited Liability Corporation, an LLC that was formed in Barbados. I'm looking into the records in Barbados to find the owner of the LLC."

"It sounds like a you're following a single strand in a bowl of spaghetti," Alice said with a laugh.

Skip smiled. "I'm having fun. This is what the job is all about." He folded up his papers and told her he would keep digging. "There's one other interesting thing about the LLC account at Butterfield that I'm still trying to unwind. Despite all those deposits over the years, there is very little money in the account, less than fifty thousand. Almost all the funds have been transferred monthly to a charity here in the U.S."

Alice tilted her head slightly to the side before asking, "What charity?"

"The Cystic Fibrosis Foundation."

***

After getting airborne, Orv turned to the southeast and crossed Highway 1 at Saddlebunch Keys. Climbing to five thousand feet, he pulled the throttle back to save fuel. The GPS updated with his new speed and calculated one hour and thirty-two minutes of remaining flight time. He started to recalculate the plane's approximate fuel burn rate based on his guess of how much fuel he had remaining but then set his calculator aside. The numbers were all presumptions; he would either make it or he would end up in the waters off Cuba.

He remembered how Alice would get so frustrated with him for calculating everything. He wasn't as bad as he used to be. When they were married, he would total the grocery bill in his head as they put items in the cart. When they drove somewhere, he would update her along the way with their estimated arrival time. He loved figures and estimates; they had always been an integral part of his career as a pilot and they naturally bled into his private life.

As he flew towards a new life, he thought about the things he was leaving behind. Nothing material that he left mattered. His apartment was bare except for a few pieces of furniture, his car was an old pile of junk. Everything that meant anything to him he carried in his backpack. His only keepsakes were a couple of letters Alice wrote him while he was in Vietnam and a small photo album. The album contained a picture of his parents and his grandparents, and he kept a picture of the two women he had loved: Alice and his baby Jessica. He wore his father's watch, and he loved his old plane, but he had never gathered anything else that was worth keeping.

The winds had calmed and the turbulence had lightened, giving him time to think about his past, about his future, and about her. In the corner of his mind, he had always held a little fantasy about bumping into Alice. They would grab a cup of coffee, reconcile the past, forgive, forget, and maybe even make plans to see each other again. That would never happen in Cuba, or St. Lucia, or wherever this journey was leading him. His past was shady, his future was unclear. He didn't know what he was flying towards.

***

After Skip Bowman left her office, Alice placed a call down to Lacy Martin in the accounting department. Lacy had mentioned in casual conversation once that she had worked in accounting for the American Lung

Association. Fifteen minutes later, Lacy stepped into Alice's office.

"What can I do for you?" asked the young accountant from Alice's office door.

Alice smiled. "I have a theoretical question. Would it be possible to launder money through a large charity, one like the Lung Association or the Cystic Fibrosis Foundation?"

Lacy thought about it for a moment. "Possible? Sure, it could be done, but those larger organizations have so many checks and balances, they have to report everything. It would be really tough."

"How would you do it?" asked Alice in a challenging tone.

Lacy slowly walked towards her desk as she thought. She sat in one of the chairs opposite the older investigator. "If dirty money was donated, and then that money was used to fund research, the researchers could be bogus..." she said as she thought out loud. "Or if donated funds were used to buy goods and services from a company owned by the same group that was donating the money, that might work. Either way would involve a lot of collusion from within the charity."

Alice cut to the point. "I've got a known drug dealer who makes regular payments to an account in the Cayman Islands. We suspect that those funds are paid to the people who transport the drugs by boat or plane. When we unwound that account, we found that the account owner has been donating a majority of the funds to the Cystic Fibrosis Foundation here in the U.S. How do we figure out the money laundering trail from here?"

Lacy had a confused look on her face. "Your mule is donating all of the profits to Cystic Fibrosis?"

"Yes," said Alice. "Is that the best use of drug money you've ever heard?"

Lacy laughed. "If we could get them all to participate like that, we'd be a disease-free society in about six months." She looked out the window for a few moments before continuing. "I guess the next step is to start an investigation into the Foundation's books. How much money are we talking about?"

"Skip Bowman is still trying to get the account records, but it looks like an average of eighteen thousand dollars a week has been transferred to the CF Foundation for the last two years."

Lacy looked at the ceiling. "Eighteen thousand over fifty weeks a year for two years is…one point eight million dollars?"

"Yeah," replied Alice.

"That's not a generous donor. That's a money-laundering scheme," stated Lacy in an upbeat tone.

Alice smiled at her enthusiasm. "Have you ever considered a career in our forensic accounting department?"

"And give up all the glamour of payroll and expense accounts?" asked Lacy, her question dripping with sarcasm.

***

A little wave of relief rushed over Orv when he spotted the clouds that often rose over Cuba's San Miguel Mountain Range. Fifteen minutes later, he could make out Cayo Cruz de Padre, the westernmost of the Santa Clara bay islands. He had purposely flown west of his GPS course to find the bay. It was a longer route to Isabela but safer. If the big fan on the front of the plane quit turning, he would be over the bay, close to the islands, and much more likely to successfully dead-stick his plane into the calmer waters.

Maintaining five thousand feet gave him enough glide path to give him options. He flew down the length of Cayo Ranas and Cayo Cabenzos, both islands he hoped to explore more in the near future. Over Mahomito, he spotted the Isabela Peninsula. His engine ran smoothly, despite his gauges indicating his tanks were empty. He was on fumes. He stayed high, leaving a multitude of landing options available to him until he had flown past the peninsula and made his base turn. Then he pulled back the throttle to idle and bled off his altitude to maintain his speed as he turned back to the west on his final approach. To keep from attracting any unwanted attention from the Cuban Air Defense, he didn't radio his intentions. Instead, he kept a sharp eye out for any other aircraft.

Isabela de Sagua, known to the locals simply as Isabela, had also been nicknamed La Venecia de Cuba, or The Venice of Cuba. It was a beautiful little village on the end of a tiny spit of land that jutted out of Cuba's northern coast. The little fishing village held only a few thousand inhabitants, two restaurants, and a cozy, comfortable hotel.

Orv had first come to the village when he was a co-pilot for the Flying Tigers Freight Line. Unable to fly directly from the U.S. because of the existing trade embargo, Flying Tigers would fly to points in Cuba from the Bahamas or Jamaica. One trip, they experienced a mechanical problem after landing at Able Santamaria and had to wait a day for the company to fly in parts and mechanics. Orv borrowed a motorcycle and went exploring and had fallen in love with the little village that was surrounded by water.

On approach, he weighed his options. He wanted to land as close to the village as possible. It would be horrible to run out of fuel while taxiing in and have to wave down a boat to rescue him. But he also knew that many of the locals put out crab and lobster traps close to shore. Hitting a trap line at sixty or eighty miles an hour could tear a float off or cause a ground loop on the water, both which were deadly. He would have to chance landing further out and hoping he made it to the docks on the eastern side of the peninsula.

The waters in the lee of the spit were calm. He set the plane down easily on the harbor and felt her sink in as she slowed. Orv listened intently for a cough, a sputter, anything signaling him she was about to run out of gas, but the old Beaver kept chugging away.

Four kids excitedly ran down to the dock near the Vista al Mar restaurant. He eased her up to the dock and signaled for them to grab the short rope that hung from the end of the wing. As if they had done it before, they held the plane in place long enough for him to get out and grab the line off the front of the port float and secure it to the dock.

"Gracias," he said. They excitedly asked him questions in Spanish as he secured the rear of the float. "No Espanol," he said, using the remaining Spanish he knew. Reaching into his pocket, he stripped off four American dollars from his wad and handed them each one. As they marveled over the bills they each held in their hands, he used his best sign language to tell them to watch the plane and he would give them more.

With his security team in place, he locked the plane and walked ashore. A few doors over from the dock, he entered the familiar Vista al Mar restaurant, where he was happy to see his friend Tomas behind the bar. His only customer was a redheaded woman, who, in this remote Cuban village, stuck out like a sore thumb. She was dressed like she was going out for the evening in Miami: a tight, flowered blouse, black slacks, and a pair of four-inch heels.

"Tomas!" said Orv as he walked into the bar.

"Orville, it has been too long, my friend," replied the bartender with a big smile. "I wondered if that was you in the airplane."

The redheaded patron turned towards him. "You've created quite a stir in the village, dropping out of the sky like that. This is the most exciting thing to happen here in months," Her English was perfect despite a slight slur that he suspected came from an afternoon on the barstool. Her accent sounded American, west coast, perhaps.

"Orville, this is Miss Leah Marchbanks, from the United States. She lives near the village," said Tomas. He turned to Leah and said, "Miss Marchbanks, this is Mister Orville. He is a pilot."

"I see," said Leah. "And a very good-looking pilot too. May I buy you a drink?"

Orv smiled at the woman, who looked like a hungry cat ready to pounce. "I'll have a Cristal," he said to Tomas.

"What brings you to our little piece of paradise?" asked the woman.

"I'm just passing through," he said in hopes of discouraging her a bit.

"On your way to?" she asked.

"Anagada, the ah, British Virgin Islands," he lied. "That reminds me, Tomas. Can you call over to Santamaria and ask them to bring out a two-hundred-liter barrel of aviation fuel tomorrow?"

The bartender nodded as he set the bottle of beer in front of Orv and then wrote the fuel request on a small pad of paper.

"And what does Anagada have that we don't?" asked Leah in a sultry tone.

"Do you hit on every pilot that comes in here?" asked Orv with a bit of irritation in his voice.

"I don't know," she said with a laugh. "I've been here for months and you're the first pilot to arrive. Like I said, you're the most interesting thing that's happened here in months."

Orv took a sip of his beer. "So what's your deal? Why are you here?"

Leah leaned towards him, resting her arms on the bar and giving him a sexy, sultry look. "I'm in the witness protection program. I witnessed my husband cheating on me, and if I'm near him or his little slut again, I'll kill them both."

Orv was intrigued but also a hundred percent certain that he wanted nothing to do with the woman. She had the look of danger and the smell of trouble. She was completely out of place, an apparent woman of society, a lady who was used to money and all it implied sitting in Isabela, Cuba. "You sound like you're from California. LA?"

She smiled. "San Clemente. My great-grandfather helped develop the city back in the twenties. It was his clean canvas, five miles long, a half mile wide, his vision of eutopia."

"I've never been there," said Orv. "I've heard it's beautiful."

Leah scoffed. "It's a horrid little town where everybody knows everybody else's business. My family sits on top of the gossip chain like a cherry on an ice cream sundae. To make matters worse, my so-called husband is the president of a medical device manufacturer in town, one of the area's largest employers. We don't sneeze without half the town blessing us and the other half cussing us."

"So why are you in Isabela?" he asked.

She pointed to her drink and nodded her head towards Tomas, signaling to him that she wanted another. "My great-grandfather, after developing his nirvana by the sea, got bored and decided to grow sugar cane in Cuba. He bought a plantation just up the river in the forties. During the Cuban revolution, the Bay of Pigs, the missile crisis, and the entirety of the cold war, our little flag-waving, all-American family exported sugar and tobacco to the Soviet Union while paying exorbitant amounts of money in taxes and bribes to the Cubans."

She paused then sat up straight and tried to look professional and austere. "I'm here to look after my family's interests while plotting the death of my husband and his little tart."

Orv laughed. At another time or another place, he might be interested in her advances. But he had a lot to think about and Alice weighed heavy on his mind. He didn't need to get involved. He had a lot going on in his head. He just came here to drink.

He guessed she was a few years younger than he was, and it was apparent that she had worked hard to slow the vestiges of time from creeping up on her. Orv imagined that she worked out on a regular basis and had seen a long list of plastic surgeons, skin care specialists, and personal trainers in her past.

"You're not leaving until tomorrow," she said as Tomas delivered another drink to her and set a fresh beer in front of Orv. "Join me for dinner. Save me from my boredom, share one evening of intelligent conversation and good wine with me. I don't bite."

She made such an impassioned plea that it would have been very hard to turn her down. And, he had nothing else to do but sit in the bar and drown in his own thoughts until they kicked him out. He agreed to have dinner with her but told her flat out that it was just dinner and conversation.

"Of course," she said. "I was just being a pill earlier. I didn't mean to make you feel uncomfortable. Let's finish our drinks, then we'll drive out to the plantation. I can give you a tour while Rosa cooks us a wonderful meal."

"Let me get a room at the hotel and freshen up first," said Orv. "I can find my way out to your place."

"I wouldn't hear of it," she protested. "We have so many empty rooms at the house, you will stay there, not at the local cockroach inn."

Orv's finances were a bit up in the air, he wasn't exactly sure how much money he had in his Cayman account, he had just quit his job, and the pension he had planned to keep, he had last seen floating away off Mud Key. A free dinner and a room might not be a bad thing. He could still run pretty fast for a guy his age, but she looked like she still had some chase left in her.

***

"Do you want to see a picture of the drug plane we were looking for, the Beaver?" said Mark Young as he stepped into Alice's office early the following morning.

"Yeah!" she said excitedly. "Did you find satellite pictures?"

"No, better," said Young as he walked around her desk. "I was searching the internet for photos of de Havilland Beavers, so I could compare wing shapes, fuselage shapes, nose cones, and other distinguishing features when looking at the satellite images. As I was searching, I stumbled across a picture that a tourist posted last week."

He set a printed photo on her desk of a man in a flowered shirt standing on a beach in front of two seaplanes. The plane in the foreground was blue, yellow, and displayed "Miami Seaplanes" in large letters down its side. The plane in the background was larger, older, and a faded orange and white. The comment under the photo said, "Floyd and I having lunch at the Lorelei, two seaplanes on the beach."

"Is that a Beaver?" Alice asked Mark.

"Yeah," he said with a smile as he handed her a second photo. "But not just a Beaver, I think it's our Beaver. I blew up the photo large enough to see the tail number."

"N71WT," she read out loud. "Son of a bitch," said Alice. "And you think this was taken just the other day?"

"Yeah, it was posted on Facebook by a lady named Gloria Urbanski. She and her husband are from Michigan. They are spending a few weeks in the Keys. It was the most random find ever. I was searching Facebook, and somebody replied to her post saying the second plane was a Beaver, like the one they had flown in Alaska."

Alice reached into her desk drawer and pulled out a small magnifying glass she started keeping there when she noticed age taking her eyesight. She carefully studied both photos before asking, "Is that some sort of logo, forward of the tail number?"

"Yes, it says *Tarpon Jim Fishing Charters*. I checked them out. They went out of business years ago."

"No," said Alice, "the smaller logo, the red one."

Setting three more photos on her desk, he said, "I tried to blow it up, but the photo is just too grainy to really tell what it is. What do you see?"

Alice peered through her magnifying glass for several moments, going from one blown up photo to the next. When she realized he was right, she looked back at the original photo and with the magnification. She turned on the banker's lamp on the corner of her desk and moved the photo under it and inspected it again.

"Oh my God!" she gasped uncontrollably. She sat up straight in her chair as if she had seen a ghost in the picture. Her voice cracked as she pushed the magnifying glass and photo towards him. "What do you see?"

Mark was surprised by her expression. He watched her with a questioning look for a moment before re-inspecting the photo. Tilting the photo at an angle to the light, he finally found a position to the light and a focus that all lined up. "It looks like a heart, a broken heart. You know, the heart with the crack in it. The name on the sash across the heart looks like it says, 'Jessica.' Is that what you saw?" he asked as he looked back towards her. Alice was sitting back in her chair. She stared out the window as a single tear formed in the corner of her eye. Her face held a strange expression and had turned pale, almost ashen.

***

Orv woke, showered, pulled on his shirt and shorts, and walked to the home's huge kitchen to see if he could find a cup of coffee. He surprised the maid, who was beating some sort of batter in a bowl. "Coffee?" he asked.

"Si," she responded before wiping her hands and rushing to get the stranger a cup of coffee. She handed it to him and smiled, but he saw suspicion in her eyes.

"Senora Leah?" he asked.

The maid said something, then smiled and made a gesture with her hands, indicating that her head was resting on a pillow. Orv understood. The Senora wouldn't be up for a while. He thanked her for the coffee then stepped out onto the large veranda that dominated the north side of the home.

It was an incredible day. The sun shined across the beautiful property, a light breeze blew in from the west, and a light scent of flowers wafted in the wind. Orv guessed from the architecture that the home was built in the twenties. It had been meticulously maintained over the years. The plantation's main house and veranda overlooked the sugarcane fields in the river bottom land below. Leah had told him the plantation was over two thousand hectares in size. They had argued about the hectare to acre conversion. Orv remembered it being roughly two to one, which made the plantation four to five thousand acres.

He had enjoyed a nice evening. Leah had been on her best behavior, although she tossed out a couple of suggestive hints that were hard to miss. They sat up late and talked about her past, growing up in San Clemente, spending her summers surfing at San Onofre, and visiting her grandfather on the Cuban plantation.

He told her about his youth, then surprisingly, he told her about his time in the war. Maybe it was the wine or her gentle prodding, but he had seldom told anybody about the war. He told her about being shot down, about the evil yellow-eyed man. He even showed her the scar on his chest. He explained how his turning and involuntary ducking just before being shot caused the bullet to pass through him with minimal damage to his right lung.

Orv talked about Alice, how she had nursed him back to health, and about how they had eventually drifted apart after the failed airline deal. He didn't mention their daughter; he couldn't. Leah surprised him. She listened to his stories, she asked leading questions, and got him to talk about things he hadn't talked about in a very long time. She told him she didn't believe his story, that he was on his way to Anagada for business. He politely told her he didn't care to discuss the real reason for his trip.

When they had finished the wine and the candle on the table had burned low, Leah stood up, said goodnight to him, and left him sitting alone. He watched the moon disappear over the horizon. It had been a very pleasant evening.

***

Alice walked into Johnny Reno's office and closed the door. "Can I talk to you, completely off the record?"

He shot her a concerned look before replying, "Of course."

She sat in a chair at his desk. "I think I have a big problem."

"Oh?" replied Johnny.

"I asked you to find my ex-husband the other day and you came up with a goose egg. You said he was either a hermit, a criminal, or dead."

Johnny nodded.

"We've been digging into Angel Martin's financials. Skip found regular transfers to the Caymans, which we think could be payments to fly his drugs into the Keys," she continued. "When we researched the account receiving the funds, we found that a major portion of money was subsequently being donated to the Cystic Fibrosis Foundation in the U.S."

"Interesting," said Johnny while making a note on his yellow legal pad. He also made a mental note, that Alice hadn't been herself since the incident in Key West. She was scattered, emotional, not the rock that he had known her to be.

"We were given a tip yesterday regarding a seaplane that might be moving drugs into the Keys. The tail number and type of plane were the same that the Navy spotted during a routine flight a few days ago. We ran the tail number. It's bogus. The plane is a de Havilland Beaver floatplane, and the tail number is registered to a Cessna that we confirmed is in Texas."

Johnny made some additional notes but only offered, "Uh huh," as a response.

Alice laid a photo and a small magnifying glass on his desk. "Mark found a photo a tourist took of the Beaver on Islamorada the other day."

He picked up the photo and the magnifying glass then spent a few moments carefully examining the image. "Is that a broken heart next to a name by the ID number?" he asked.

"Yes," said Alice while wiping a tear from the corner of her eye.

"Jessica?" he asked while looking up at her.

"Yeah," she replied. "A thousand years ago, my husband and I had a daughter we named Jessica. She died of Cystic Fibrosis when she was two months old."

***

Valle de Sagua, the family's plantation, could have been mistaken for a five-star resort. Orv was doted over by the maid staff. They kept his coffee full then brought him breakfast on the veranda. The view was incredible, the eggs and sausage, fresh fruit, and pastries were the best he had enjoyed in years. They even brought him a mimosa. He was beginning to wonder why he would ever leave.

"I see you've been well taken care of," said Leah as she waked out to his table. She was dressed as though she was staying at the Ritz on St. Bart's. She wore a flower-patterned sundress and a large floppy hat; her sunglasses and shoes matched. Even in her own home, Leah dressed like a flamboyant woman of society.

"Your staff has been fabulous. They really know how to treat a guest," said Orv with a smile. "How are the mojitos?"

"They are fabulous. They make them with just the right amount of rum," said Leah as the maid came out and handed her a mimosa. Leah said something to her in Spanish, and the woman nodded and left. "Most of the staff has been here as long as I can remember. We have always paid them well." She gestured towards the maid who had just walked back into the house. "Maria has been here since I was a little girl. She doesn't seem to age. I love her and hate her all at the same time."

They sat in silence for several minutes, each sipping on their drink as they enjoyed the view and the incredibly pleasant morning. "I thought about you last night after I went to bed," said Leah, breaking the silence.

Orv smiled. "I'm not sure I want to know your thoughts. I'm a pretty modest guy."

She turned towards him. "Get over yourself. The way you spoke last night, you're so in love with your ex-wife that you wouldn't have touched me if I had attacked you."

"That was just the alcohol talking," he responded as the smile disappeared from his face. "I haven't seen her in more than ten years. I was just rehashing old memories."

"Hmm," she replied in a judgmental tone as she turned back towards the view. She remained silent for several minutes before she asked, "Are you running from her, the law, or something else?"

"I'm not running from anything," Orv protested. "I told you, I'm heading to a meeting in the BVI."

"Fine," she said. "You're under no obligation to tell me the truth."

"What makes you think I'm lying?" he asked in a contemptuous tone.

Leah smiled a slightly devious smile and took a sip of her drink. "My father was a pilot. I know a bit about flying. Your plane is sitting at the dock, out of fuel. You don't even have enough gas to safely make it to Santamaria, thirty miles inland. That means you're either the worst pilot in the world or you didn't plan to come to Cuba yesterday. Shall I go on?"

"Please," said Orv with a smile.

She finished her drink. "If you were going to Anagada, in that plane, you would have packed a few days of clothes. It's not a down and back in one day sort of trip, not in an old seaplane. All you seem to have with you is the clothes you wore yesterday and that little backpack, which probably contains your passport, a small stack of cash, your toothbrush, and a few photos of 'her'."

The only thing she left out, thought Orv, was his .45 pistol. Other than that, she had been pretty much dead-on when describing his belongings.

She knew from his silence, his lack of retort that she was right on target. She had always fancied herself as a good judge of character, except for her first two husbands, and the current one. "So," Leah asked again, "who are you running from?"

"I might have a little legal trouble back in the States," he confessed with a grimace.

She uncrossed her legs, put her elbows on the table, and leaned in close. "Oh, do tell."

"No way," said Orv. "You've been a gracious hostess, but I should probably be going now."

She put on her best pouty face. "Oh, come on. I'm so bored. Tell me what you did, let me live vicariously through you." She smiled a sexy smile. "I'll never tell."

Orv shook his head. "No, even my being here could put you in legal trouble, maybe even physical danger. You know, harboring a fugitive?" he said with a nervous chuckle.

"I told you that my family has been violating the Cuban embargo for fifty years and that I was plotting to kill my husband," she said with a smile. She could tell by looking that the man wasn't going to confess. "It's pretty evident that you're a drug runner."

He was visibly shocked that she had guessed. "Why would you think that?" he said in a slightly elevated voice.

"You arrived here in a beat-up old seaplane with a weak story," she said with a satisfied giggle. "You're armed and on the run from the law. That just smells like a drug runner."

"I'm not armed," he said in protest.

"Well no," she said with a laugh. "Not at the moment, but you have a .45 Ruger in your backpack."

"You went through my backpack?" he asked.

"No!" she said quickly. "Okay, maybe," she continued after a little giggle.

"You are a horrible person," he said with just a hint of a grin.

"I know," she said with a girlish laugh. "But I'm just a poor defenseless woman all alone in this big house."

***

Johnny Reno sat quietly while looking over his notes and the photos while pondering the information Alice had just given him. His face twisted into a pained look. "Can I be frank with you?"

She looked at him. "Of course."

"I know you want to find your ex-husband, and I see the coincidences in your case, but the whole thing is pretty thin. The airplane is suspicious, and it looks like somebody may be laundering money through a charity. But connecting your ex-husband into this case based on the fact that he's gone ghostal, and some pilot got his heart broken by a woman named Jessica, is a huge stretch."

"I would completely agree with you except," she said before putting her finger on the photo, "that is the exact tattoo my husband got on his right shoulder a few weeks after our baby died."

***

Orv and Leah drank the morning away under the shade of an umbrella on the veranda. They each had been starving for what they had shared the night before and what they shared in the shade, simple conversation. Orv's life had been very solitary over the years. Leah was in a sort of self-exile; even she couldn't explain why she was in Cuba.

Orv told her about his years of flying contraband. She thought it sounded exciting and romantic, but he told her it was just a job. He flew a noisy plane in all kinds of weather. The pungent aroma of marijuana invaded his cockpit as he evaded the Navy, the Coast Guard, the DEA, and numerous other agencies. He never knew when a fighter jet might appear off the side of his plane and order him to land, or when helicopters and high-speed boats would appear as he loaded or unloaded the goods.

He told her about landing on the water in remote areas of the Keys and the Bahamas. Every takeoff and every landing was a challenge, and the sea bucked and rolled as he coaxed the plane into the air or charmed it to land.

"Someday when I die," he told her, "a small group of pilots will gather in a little bar in North Miami and toast their fallen comrade. They will savor their whiskey while they wait their turn."

"See!" she said excitedly. "I knew you were a romantic." Orv frowned.

For the first time in months, Leah talked about her husband. She had no real friends in Cuba, and she didn't want to discuss her personal life with the staff. She found comfort in the easy-going drug pilot. She confessed that their marriage hadn't been good in years, but she had never cheated on him. When she discovered the affair, she was sick. He confessed to it but told her he had no interest in ending it or in granting her a divorce. She could simply "deal with it" or sue him for divorce, but he promised to take everything.

"Could he get everything?" asked Orv.

"No," she quickly answered. "He doesn't even know about everything, but he could make a divorce a long and nasty process. I decided to come down here for a couple of weeks to get away from the country club gossip and try to decide what to do. I've been here for three months."

"So what are you going to do?" he asked.

"The hell if I know," she replied. "Don and his little slut are probably playing house in my bed. I'm pissed off, humiliated, irritated, and full of thoughts of revenge. I guess when I feel like I can control my emotions, I'll go back to San Clemente and file for divorce."

"In the meantime," said Orv, "we can enjoy this beautiful morning and watch the sugar cane grow."

Maria appeared with another round of fresh drinks. She said something in Spanish to Leah, then turned to leave them.

"Tomas just called. The fuel for your airplane has been delivered and pumped into the tank. Do you call it a gas tank on a plane?" asked Leah.

Orv looked at his watch. "Oh shit, I forgot all about that. They fueled the plane without me paying for it?"

Leah smiled. "I'm sure Tomas vouched for you. If you're a friend of Tomas, you have instant credit anywhere in the area." The truth was, if you were a guest at *Valle de Sagua,* you had instant credit in the valley. The Brown family, over the years, had been so fair and honest with the locals, in their dealings and their employment, that nobody questioned them or their guests. If the plane took off and flew away without paying for the fuel, they knew somebody at the plantation would pay for their guest's blunder.

Orv leaned back in his chair with his fresh drink in hand. "I'm not flying anywhere today," he said as he slightly raised his cocktail to her. "Would it be okay if I spent another night?"

"It would be my pleasure," said Leah with a smile.

CHAPTER EIGHT

Losing a large load of product was a huge financial blow to Angel and his business, but losing his pilot was a much greater loss. Orv had been as reliable as a good watch. He had never missed a flight. He had performed so well, he had been so honest, that Angel believed that he must have crashed.

He had successfully delivered the first shipment of cash from John's sales on the mainland to the Bahamas; not a penny was missing. Then, according to his boat captain in the Bahamas, he had loaded twenty-nine bags of Columbian and took off but never arrived in the Keys. If he had been caught by the authorities, Angel would have heard about it. Stealing the weed didn't make any sense. It would have made more sense to steal the cash rather than the pot that he would have to sell.

The loss of the most reliable pilot he had ever employed was a blow to the gut. Angel had just started selling on the mainland, he was moving more product than ever, and now his supply line was severed. He scrambled to find some way to move huge amounts of pot to the islands, but it wasn't as if he could post a classified ad. Angel instructed his associate to book the next available flight for the two of them to Miami.

Five minutes after booking the flights, the DEA knew his plans. Thirty minutes after that, Tom Eason and his colleagues knew Angel was flying in from San Juan.

***

Alice sat at her desk and blindly stared at the wall on the far side of her office. In one respect, she was happy to know that Orv was alive, and still doing what he loved most, flying. But the little detail that he was flying drugs obscured most of her warm feelings. She wanted to scream at him for the lives he ruined, she wanted to slap him for all the human wreckage that his cargo created.

Seeing the broken heart with the white banner across it that bore Jessica's name brought back so many memories. Alice couldn't keep them at bay this time. She couldn't suppress them, and part of her didn't want to try.

Her career at the DEA would be impacted when he was caught. She wasn't likely to be fired because her ex-husband was indicted as a major drug trafficker, but it would forever haunt her within the agency. Alice would always be the agent who had been married to the contraband pilot. The stigma would be with her forever. There would be an investigation to see if there was any collusion between them. She would be found innocent, but they would all believe what they wanted to believe.

Her mind raced back to the good years. The first memories to surface, the most vivid were of their laughter. She remembered the beach and the ocean. Orv loved to be near the water. Every now and then, he would sneak her aboard one of his cargo flights to some far-flung island in the Caribbean. They would escape for a few hours to an amazing beach during the downtime, when Orv should have been sleeping. Together they would play in the warm waters and bask on the white sands, they would laugh and make love. She would never forget the laughter and being near the ocean with Orv.

"Do you have a moment?" asked Mark Young from her office door.

She waved him in. "What do you have?" she asked, seeing the papers in his hand.

"Satellite images from two weeks ago," said Young as he walked around her desk. "I've been going through a lot of images. It's amazing how many times this particular satellite passes over Miami in the dark or on cloudy days. But two weeks ago, it captured this photo of Watson Island."

She inspected the photo; her eyes went to the seaplane base, where she could clearly see five planes sitting on the tarmac and one on the water just off the ramp. To her untrained eye, all she could see was the aerial view, the top down picture of six planes, six sets of wings. "Tell me what I'm seeing," she said after inspecting the photo for a moment.

"Look at the size of the wings," Young said. "The Beaver was designed as a bush plane, short take-off and landings. It was built to be the pickup truck of the sky, able to haul heavy loads in to places with short runways, or no runways at all. To get the kind of lift they needed, the engineers at de Havilland built it with huge wings. See the one plane that doesn't match the others? That aircraft's wings and the shape of the tail all match the Beaver. I'm confident that is our plane."

Alice examined the photo for several more seconds. "That man told us he hadn't seen the Beaver since April."

"Should we take these photos over there and ask him what kind of plane that is?" asked Young.

She let out a long sigh while thinking through a strategy. "No, the manager is a pretty cool customer. If we showed him a picture of himself standing next to the Beaver, he would believably deny it. Let's pull over one of his young employees and put the fear of God into them. One of those kids we saw standing around, they might talk if they think they are going to jail for harboring a drug smuggler."

"It's not legal and probably not admissible in court," Young reminded her.

"I don't give a damn," she said. "We need to confirm that the plane was there and see if we can get the name of the pilot."

Young nodded. She was his superior and if that was the way she wanted to play it, he would go along with her. He had no idea of her real motivations.

***

After a pleasant alcohol-induced afternoon nap, Orv woke to find a small pile of neatly folded clothes on the dresser in his room that hadn't been there when he went to sleep. Some little fairy had delivered a couple of pairs of Bermuda shorts and a couple of shirts, all button-up short sleeve. Taking the hint, he selected a pair of tan shorts and a cream-colored shirt. After slipping them on, he looked in the mirror and smiled. Then he removed the shirt, went into the bathroom, and shaved.

Once presentable, he decided to take a quick walk to help him wake up. East of the main house were a number of buildings, equipment sheds, a paddock that was empty but likely held horses at some point, and some small houses. Two little girls played a game in front of one of the houses. They were surprised by his appearance, and despite his friendliest smile, they ran to the door and watched him pass with great suspicion.

Orv correctly suspected that the five little homes were staff housing. Behind the houses was a large, well-kept garden that obviously supplied the plantation with a majority of their vegetables. Beyond the houses and sheds, down the hill a few hundred yards, he came across a large field, perhaps twenty acres of what he suspected was tobacco. Beyond that, he could see fruit trees, and across the road, to the south, he saw rows of grapes, a small vineyard. He was impressed by the self-containment of the little plantation.

He arrived back at the main house and retreated to the shade of the veranda. Seconds after taking his chair in the shade, Maria appeared and asked him, using mostly sign language, if he was hungry or wanted a drink. Using his best broken Spanish, he asked for some water and a little snack. "Agua e pequeno comida."

She nodded then disappeared back into the house. He didn't know what to expect, his memory of the language was so bad that he wouldn't be surprised if she came back with an elephant and a large wrench. He was happy when she returned with a large glass of water and a plate of yuca chips, a Cuban favorite that he had enjoyed before.

After Orv had finished the entire plate of chips and the glass of water, Leah appeared. "I see you've started happy hour without me," she said with a smile and a wink.

"No, Ma'am," Orv retorted. "I was just enjoying some water and a snack. Thank you, by the way, for the loan of the clothes."

"You're welcome," she said. "This has been such a male-dominated house for the last five or six decades that it was easy to find some things I thought would fit you. You look very nice," she added with a smile.

Orv sort of blushed then finished his water.

"If you've had enough to tide you over until dinner, let's go for a drive," she said. "I've asked Alejandro to bring the car up. I'll show you around a bit."

Orv nodded in agreement then stood to follow her. As they walked out the massive twin front doors and down the stairs that led to the circular drive, an absolutely stunning car came around the corner and pulled up on in front of them.

"No way!" exclaimed Orv. "Is that really what I think it is?"

Leah smiled but didn't answer. She could see his overwhelming appreciation for the car and decided to let him drool for a few minutes.

"Is this real?" he asked. "A Cord Boattail Speedster?" He carefully approached the car as she watched from the stairs.

The car was decked out in white with black fenders and trunk, the black swooped forward towards the dramatically raked windshield. She looked like she was wearing a tuxedo. Auburn, Duesenberg, Packard, and others all built models similar to the dramatic speedster in the 1930s, but they were all based on the Cord. Designed to look like an open cockpit airplane without wings, she sat low and long. A narrow grille and hood widened in flowing lines back to the passenger doors, then came together in a point at the trunk, hence the look of a boat tail of the day. Huge external fenders covered each gangster whitewall tire.

Alejandro, the plantation's mechanic, didn't speak English. He didn't need to know a single word to understand the stranger's excitement over the car. He opened the hood to let him see the original L-29 Lycoming motor, he encouraged him run his hands over the soft leather seats and proudly showed him the custom woodwork on the dash. Orv told the man that it was the most beautiful thing he had ever seen. Alejandro understood.

"Greta Garbo purchased her new from the factory," said Leah as Orv drooled on the old car. "Garbo brought it to Cuba on the ferry in the late 30s. My grandfather bought the car from her in the early 1950s. He loved the car but eventually parked it in one of the sheds down below, where it sat for a long time. When we hired Alejandro fifteen years ago, he found it and asked if he could restore it. My father told him to do it, not knowing that it would take him ten years to complete the project. He did it in his spare time, and getting parts wasn't easy."

"It's incredible. I never imagined something so fantastic could be here in Cuba," said Orv with slightly glazed over eyes.

"The car officially belongs to the family," she continued. "But she's Alejandro's baby. He will let us take her out for a spin if you promise to be very careful."

"I'm not driving," Orv protested weakly.

Alejandro opened the driver's side door and motioned for Orv to get in. Orv tried not to rush at the opportunity. After he was seated, the Cuban mechanic rushed to the passenger's side and opened the door for the lady. Then they had a brief conversation in Spanish.

"He would like me to remind you that it is a very old car. It has hydraulic brakes that don't stop like modern cars, and the transmission is not synchromesh. You will need to shift carefully until you get the hang of it. I assured him that you fly aircraft worth much more than this silly old car, but he insisted that I tell you of the car's intricacies."

Orv turned to the man while he gently petted the steering wheel. "My bambina," he said, indicating to the mechanic that he would take very good care of his baby.

After grinding the gears shifting from first to second, Orv got the hang of it. He had to shift slowly, feeling when the gears were lined up instead of slamming the transmission into gear as he was used to on modern cars. Before they made it to the main road, he tested the brakes a few times. It was clear they were not modern power brakes. Every ounce of stopping power came from his leg.

On the main road, Orv accelerated and shifted gently, trying to get the feel for the automobile. He was instantly underwhelmed by the performance of a car that he had lusted over for years. The Cord was a heavy car, built before manufacturers were concerned about fuel economy. The Lycoming eight-cylinder motor only produced 125 horsepower. The brakes were the same used on tractors of the day and the steering was all muscle. Then he reminded himself, that in 1930, the car was only owned by millionaires and movie stars. It was the hottest and most innovative sportscar on the road. She was one of the first front-wheel-drive cars ever produced. Her independent suspension was revolutionary. He looked down the long hood and smiled. Very few people, then or now, were lucky enough to drive such a car.

"We'll go about two miles down here and I'll show you where to turn. There is a great swimming hole we used to ride horses to when we were kids," Leah said. "Then we can drive up and see the waterfall."

She looked at the pilot sitting next to her and silently sighed. With the clean clothes and the shave, his natural good looks were much more apparent. He cleaned up well. Orv had a polite southern charm about him that she found very attractive. She could imagine herself with such a man but hearing him speak of his ex-wife made her believe his heart was still taken.

"Tell me about her," said Leah.

"About who?" asked Orv, but he knew to whom she was referring.

"Tell me about your ex-wife."

Orv thought about Alice for a few moments in silence. He remembered her smile, her laugh; everything that came to his mind was good and pleasant. "She was my first love. We met in school. I thought she was the most beautiful girl I had ever seen. After high school, we went to college together. She wanted to be a lawyer and then a judge, but I wanted to fly. The cheapest way to learn to fly was in the military, so I joined the Army. After I was injured, I was shipped back to the States. Alice put everything on hold to take care of me. As far as I know, she never finished school to become a lawyer."

Orv laughed then turned towards Leah. "Do you know what she was doing the last time I spoke with her? She was working narcotics for the Dade County Sheriff's Department."

Leah laughed out loud then pointed to their turn. Orv slowed the car and crept along the dirt road to the swimming hole, trying not to get the Cord too dusty. He didn't want to anger Alejandro.

After a minute of reflection, he said, "I said good-bye to Alice after our divorce was final. I turned my back and walked away from her hoping it would all work out somehow."

Leah silently wondered what it took to make him run away from her.

"It would be interesting to see her now," he said quietly. "To see her without all the emotion and the pain, to see her with my wise and steady eyes." He looked far down the road and said, "I wonder how it would be to see her now."

***

Poorly conceived plans were the quickest to put into place. Alice was acting more out of emotion than logic, she knew it, but she didn't care. With Agent Young at her side, they drove out to the Seaplane Base at five in the afternoon and waited in the parking lot for one of the kids to get off work. Twenty minutes after arriving, a long-haired kid wearing a blue company tee-shirt slowly walked out of the hangar building and got into a beat-up Nissan pickup. "That's our target," said Alice.

They followed the kid across the causeway and back towards town. When he exited the 395 at 17th Avenue, Alice nodded and Young turned on the red and blue emergency lights hidden in the grille of the otherwise nondescript sedan. The kid turned the corner on to NW 6th Street and pulled over. They could see him waving around in the cab, like he was trying to shoo a bee out of the car.

The moment she stepped from her side of the car, Alice could smell the weed. The kid had fired up a joint after leaving work. She smiled and cautiously walked up to the right rear corner of the truck as Young approached the driver's side of the pickup.

"DEA," said Young with his hand on his service pistol that was holstered under his shoulder. "Please step from the vehicle." The kid complied, getting out with a defeated look on his face. "Please step to the curb," said Young, pointing towards the sidewalk.

"Please put your hands behind your back," said Alice as the kid came within arm's reach of her. She handcuffed him and asked him to sit lean against their car, where Young patted him down and searched his pockets.

"What did I do?" asked the kid.

"Well," Young laughed, "smoking a joint on your way home from work is a crime. Let's start there and we'll see how many crimes we can add to that. Word on the street is that you've been dealing."

"I don't deal," said the kid. "You've got the wrong guy!" he protested.

Young realized they didn't even know the kid's name. "Do you have some ID?"

"My wallet is in the truck," he said.

It took Young less than thirty seconds to find the kid's wallet and a baggie of joints he had stashed under the seat. Alice played her part; she stood nearby, keeping a close watch over the kid but remained completely silent.

"Well, Fredrick Bartholomew Jackson," said Young as he held up the tiny bag of pot. "This and the other evidence we have is probably enough to send you away for about ten years."

"What other evidence?" asked the kid.

Alice could see he was getting emotional. He was scared. She stepped forward. "We know a de Havilland Beaver comes in about once a week full of marijuana. And we know you and your buddies at the base are the ones dealing it all over town. They've already confessed and sold you out."

Freddy Jackson could see his future quickly slipping away. He envisioned life in prison and it scared him. Tears started to well up in his eyes. "I've never sold any dope in my entire life. I smoke a joint now and then. You got to believe me."

He was the perfect mark, Alice thought. He was scared and emotional, he was envisioning his life slipping away from him. "What's the name of the Beaver pilot?" she asked.

"I don't know," said the kid with a tear streaming down his cheek. "They call him Orv."

***

After a stop at the old swimming hole, a wonderfully inviting wide spot in the river that included a tire swing and some daring rocks to jump from, they drove a few miles further south. After passing through the little town of Sagua La Grande, they stopped at the waterfalls. A mile off the paved road, the Sagua River tumbled over a small uplift. The falls weren't dramatic, but the vegetation around the falls, created by the constant mist of the tumbling water, made a compact but magical area.

As they walked, Leah pointed out plants that were indigenous to only that spot on the island. Plants typically only found in rain forests thrived in the little biosphere below the waterfall.

Driving back to the plantation, Orv noticed people staring and waving at them. The young people stopped and gazed as the unique old car drove by, the older residents of the area waved when the recognized the Cord, which they hadn't seen in years.

"You certainly seem to be popular with the locals," said Orv as two older women waved at them enthusiastically.

Leah smiled. "The reason the plantation has survived and remained in our family's name is because my great-grandfather and my grandfather both understood how to take care of people. They took good care of the employees and they invested in the schools and churches of the nearby towns. During the revolution, my grandfather played both sides of the conflict. The family was friends with General Batista, but my grandfather also became friendly with Castro.

"When Castro proclaimed himself Prime Minister of Cuba, or president, or whatever, he claimed all property for Socialist Cuba and started shaping the country using the Soviet model. The plantation was officially taken over by the government. Luckily, pressure from the local officials and some political maneuvering by grandfather led to the state pretty much leaving us to operate and profit from the plantation as we always had. Although we paid exorbitant taxes.

"In the mid-seventies, Castro used our plantation as a pawn in a political ploy to get Cuba re-admitted to the Organization of American States. He showed Kissinger how foreign interests, specifically American interests, could survive and thrive in Cuba. The American government didn't want anybody to know that our family was making money in Cuba. They had convinced the public that the embargo was effective, so they brushed the whole matter under the rug and admitted Cuba back into the OAS. Castro felt like he owed us something for our part in his little charade, so he re-granted us permanent ownership of the land and lowered both the property and income taxes."

"Wow," said Orv. "Did you ever meet Castro?"

"Yeah, he has been to the plantation many times. My grandfather never thought much of him, but I always thought he was charming and funny."

"Your family has quite a history here," said Orv.

Leah smiled and waved at some old men sitting on a bench in front of a little cantina. They waved back, and one tipped his hat to her. "We've been down here a long time."

***

Alice didn't know what to do. She was so consumed and overwhelmed with emotions that indecision simply took over. She didn't know if she should tell her superior what she knew or, like Johnny had advised, let it play out. Neither Mark Young nor Johnny Reno would throw her under the bus. They had both heard what she suspected, that her ex-husband was the pilot they were looking for, but she knew that they would act appropriately surprised when that revelation came to light.

She decided to wait a few days before telling her boss. Perhaps her plane would crash on her way to the interagency meeting in Key West in a few days, then she wouldn't have to tell him what she knew.

Her team was in place to trail Angel Moritz when he arrived in a few hours. They would call her with any updates, but they were only to follow him and see who he came in contact with. She didn't expect to hear any reports until morning. She packed up her laptop and stepped out of her office, announcing to those on her team that still remained at their desks that she was going home. They all looked at her like the earth had stopped. As long as she had been in the department, she had always been the last to leave.

***

Angel and his associate Ezequiel Soto, who went by the nickname Rocky because he thought it sounded tough, arrived at Miami International on the early evening flight. They had a large reception committee, but the two Puerto Ricans didn't know it.

Tom Eason's men were there and also two undercover agents with the DEA. As Angel and Rocky walked towards the airport exit, four men in separate two teams, each unaware of the other, followed. As they approached the taxi stand at the curb, one of Eason's men jammed a taser into Rocky's lower back while another stuck a gun into Angel's side and told him to get into the SUV that arrived with perfect timing. The SUV pulled away unseen while the shocked people in the taxi line focused on the convulsing man on the ground. Even the DEA agents following them didn't see what had happened.

"I don't know what happened," said Agent Jeff Tunison on the phone to Alice. "They got to the taxi line, then Soto hit the ground and Moritz disappeared. Soto's on his way to the hospital. We don't know where Moritz went."

"Shit," Alice said out loud. Over the last several days, cussing had become quite a habit.

***

Arriving back at the plantation at twilight, Leah pointed the way to the building they called the shop. The building sat next to an even larger building that Leah said was the hangar. "My father had it built to house his plane. We still mow the grass strip, but I don't know why. Nobody has landed here since my father sold his plane."

"How long is the strip?" asked Orv.

"Four thousand feet," she said. "I only know that because I heard my father say it so many times."

"You've got a three-quarter-of-a-mile-long strip here at the plantation?"

Leah nodded and pointed towards the shop building. The large doors stood open and the lights were on. "Stop here," she said, indicating to park outside the building. "Alejandro doesn't allow anybody to drive the cars inside. He's afraid we might bump one of his babies into another."

Inside the large building, Orv saw a stunning display of chrome and shiny paint. "Oh my God, I have got to go see," he said while turning off the Cord's ignition.

The family's collection was impressive. Inside the shop were eleven cars, each parked at an angle facing the door. He recognized several of the American cars but was less familiar with some of the European vehicles. He looked like a kid in a candy store as Leah looked on.

"I'll leave you here with Alejandro," she said. "Come up to the house when you're hungry."

Orv and the mechanic didn't speak the same primary language, but they both spoke the universal language of cars. Alejandro showed him the 1955 Mercury pickup, painted in its original red and black color scheme. He showed him the 1941 Chrysler Town and Country woody station wagon. At the back of the wagon, he pushed out his stomach like a pregnant woman and said, "Bambino" while pointing to the rounded back of the car. The woodwork on the car was impressive.

They stopped next to the 1948 Ferrari roadster, which Alejandro explained was very fast but also used his hands to explain that it was very squirrely. The tan leather seats were some of the softest leather Orv had ever touched. There was a 1957 Chevy Bel Air convertible with the continental kit, and a 1932 Mercedes limousine that had an exposed driver's cockpit. Every car in the building was perfect. Alejandro then led him through a door in the back of the building to a large shop where the project cars were being worked on. The shop was equipped with every type of equipment he could imagine. Orv thought he had died and gone to heaven.

***

Tom Eason tried at first to reason with his guest at an empty warehouse in West Miami. He invited Angel into the office and asked him to sit. He offered him a drink and shared some cordial conversation. Then he explained to Angel that there must be some misunderstanding, because everything north of Marathon was his territory. He explained that his group had never sold south of there, and out of respect, they never would. Angel mistook Eason's soft approach as weakness and told him that he planned to take over much of the area, but also out of respect, he would not sell in Miami.

From that point on, the conversation went poorly...for Angel. Eason's men knocked out a few of his teeth, they broke his nose, and three of the fingers on his right hand. They dropped him back at the airport after making it perfectly clear that if they ever saw him, his bodyguard, or his dealer north of Marathon again, they would kill them. Angel didn't know or care where Rocky or John were; he bought a ticket on the last flight to Puerto Rico and vowed to himself to never return to the States again.

CHAPTER NINE

Leah didn't see Orv that evening. She suspected he was playing cars with her mechanic. The next morning, she was surprised to not find him sitting on the veranda. Maria told her he had woken early, grabbed a roll and a coffee, and left for the shop.

Alejandro was thrilled to have somebody around the plantation who was enthusiastic about the cars. Orv was a reasonably knowledgeable mechanic, but his real skills lay around his problem-solving abilities. Alejandro showed him a 1928 Norton CS1 motorcycle he had been restoring and told Orv with a frustrated tone, "No go." The pilot sat on a stool and stared at the bike for several minutes then picked up a small wrench and reversed the coil wires. It started on the third kick. Orv had never seen a 1928 Norton in his life, but after a few minutes, he realized there was no spark. When he sat quietly and looked over the bike, he figured that if the ignition coil was good, that must be the issue.

He soon found himself elbow deep in a 1953 Cadillac Eldorado. His new friend had asked him to remove the seats. While he crawled around the floor of the old car, he started to think about his future. He had nowhere to go and nowhere to be. Maybe Leah would hire him to help out around the place. He could work for peanuts, really just room and board, and the plantation even had a hangar with a tall enough door for a Beaver on floats. A part of him regretted telling her that he was a fugitive. It wasn't something he would tell most prospective employers. Part of him was glad she knew.

The day flew by. Before he knew it, Alejandro was putting away his tools and washing his hands. The sun was setting, and Orv realized he was starving.

He found Leah sitting on the veranda. A fresh, untouched drink sat on the table in front of her, and her head lay back against the chair. She looked concerned, even distraught, as if she was on the edge of tears.

"Is everything okay?" Orv asked in a concerned voice.

"I just got a call from my aunt. She's a mess. My uncle had a heart attack this afternoon. I need to get to Key West."

A trip to Key West from Cuba wasn't easy. It was either a boat ride across the 90-mile-wide Florida Strait or a series of commercial flights. Havana offered air service to only two cities in North America: Toronto, Canada and Mexico City. Leah could fly from Santa Clara to Havana, to Toronto, to Miami, and then to Key West. If everything was on time, if nothing went wrong, it was possible to make it in two days.

Without thinking through the ramifications, Orv blurted out to his generous hostess, "I can fly you there first thing in the morning."

A wave of relief swept over Leah's face. "Would you? I didn't want to ask, but it would be such a help. My aunt has no family in Florida. She really needs somebody there with her."

"I'd be happy to take you," said Orv as he started to think through the logistics and possible consequences of returning to the Keys. He realized that he might have spoken too quickly, but he wasn't going to take it back now.

Alice woke early, showered, dressed, and made it to the office before seven. She wanted to go over her notes for the meeting and make sure she came across as well-prepared. Their forty-minute flight out of the nearby Palm Beach airport was scheduled for nine thirty, giving her plenty of time to make sure she was organized and ready. She assembled her team in the conference room at eight-thirty and quickly went over each person's part in the meeting. Alice was proud of them. They were a good bunch of hard working, dedicated professionals.

At ten minutes after nine, they left the office for the DEA hangar on the southeast corner of the field in two separate cars. Most of her team had never flown on the department's Beechcraft King Air. It was a much different experience than flying commercial. They parked at the hangar, walked through the building, out onto the tarmac, and climbed aboard the plane. There was no security, no lines, and no waiting for boarding announcements. They went from their car seats to their airplane seats in less than three minutes.

Once on board, the pilot climbed up the stairs and pulled the door shut behind him. He pointed out the location of the lifejackets and asked them to buckle up. Two minutes later, the propellers were spinning and they began to taxi. It was the only way to fly.

***

Orv woke and had a quick breakfast. He had agreed to meet Leah at the Able Santamaria airport where he would fuel. That gave Leah a little more time to pack and say goodbye to her staff. Leah asked Alejandro to meet Orv in front of the house for a ride to his plane. He had hoped to see some fantastic classic car waiting to whisk him away. Instead, a rusty, beat-up Peugeot 405 sedan sat in the drive.

He was sure, despite its looks, that mechanically, it would get him where he needed to go.

After a quick drive to the restaurant, Alejandro walked with him out on the dock. Orv could tell the mechanic was excited to see his old plane and its large radial engine. Alejandro helped him spin the plane around, facing it out towards the open water. From the airplane, Orv retrieved a glass cylinder and inserted it into a fuel port on the bottom of the wing. After filling it with fuel, he showed Alejandro how he tested the fuel for water or other contaminants. He seldom tested the fuel he received from the Seaplane Base in Miami, but he wasn't sure of the quality delivered by the barrel in Cuba.

Confident he had good fuel on board, Orv crawled up the strut ladder and told his friend, "Mi returno." He was sure his Spanish was not correct, but the message seemed to get across that he would be back.

After pumping the wobbler pump several times to prime the engine, he hit the starter button. The engine caught with a puff of oily smoke after a few spins. Alejandro released his hold on the line attached to the front of the float and waved goodbye. As Orv taxied out into the channel, he pulled on his headset and dialed up the correct frequency for the tower at Able Santamaria Airport near Santa Clara. As soon as he was airborne, he contacted the tower and indicated his intentions to land there.

It was a very short, very routine flight. The he flew to the west a few miles, climbing to three thousand feet before turning due south. Shortly after his turn, the air traffic controller instructed him to intercept the ILS, the Instrument Landing System signal, which lined him up on the proper runway. Minutes later, he flared the plane slightly and sat it down on the runway.

His timing couldn't have been worse. Just before he landed, the Regional Administrator for Aduana General De

La Repubica, or Cuban Customs, had arrived at Able Santamaria for his monthly inspection. Standing on the tarmac, everybody turned to see the funny-looking plane on floats land on runway 26. The first letter on the tail number, the "N" indicated the aircraft was registered in the United States. The inspector pointed to the aircraft as it turned off the runway and told staff that they may as well inspect that plane first.

Orv was surprised when two cars full of uniformed officers pulled up to his plane as he shut down his engine in the transient parking area.

The men were polite but firm. Orv produced his forged U.S. passport and pilot's license. They asked to see his entry visa, which he tried to explain he did not have but would apply for immediately. Two men crawled up and began searching the plane, immediately finding both the pistol in his backpack and the AR-15 that was strapped to the bulkhead behind the pilot's seat, weakly hidden under his flight jacket.

Several sets of suspicious eyes were looking him up and down when Leah pulled up in a Land Rover and hopped out with a huge smile. She threw her arms into the air saying, "Colonel Lazarus! Es un honor que vengas a verme dejar."

She then turned to Orv, saying, "Dear, would you get my bags out of the car? I would love to stay and visit, but we really must be going."

Leah walked to the colonel and offered her hand, which the man accepted and kissed lightly. As Orv watched, the two of them had a brief conversation. Colonel Lazarus smiled, bowed his head slightly towards Leah, then motioned for his men to leave as a fuel truck pulled up beside the plane. The colonel returned Orv's passport to him, and the two men in the plane crawled down, leaving the guns where they found them before they hurried to the cars.

"What did you say to him?" asked Orv as he watched them leave. Only a minute earlier, he thought he was going to spend the rest of his life in a Cuban prison.

"I told the colonel it was an honor to have him come out to see me off," she said with a smile.

Orv shook his head and laughed. "How much weight does your family pull around here? A simple wave from you and customs and weapon charges simply go away?"

Leah smiled. "I've heard the term 'Castro's Americanos' used to describe our family. I guess the good colonel is familiar with that term too."

***

The flight from Palm Beach to Key West was mercifully short. A van had been arranged to drive the group from the airport to the Fairfield Inn, on the north side of the island where the meetings were to be held.

The meeting rooms had been set up just as requested. Alice opened the day with an all-inclusive meeting, an introduction to the "new DEA" and an overview of the cooperative plan they would be introducing throughout the day. After introducing all the players, they disbursed into smaller breakout sessions to discuss different aspects of the plan, including air and sea intercepts, intelligence gathering, undercover infiltration, and Navy and Coast Guard participation.

During a break, Monroe County Deputy Eubanks caught Alice. "We have a new development. Angel Moritz was using a new guy to deal here and up on the mainland, a guy we knew here as John. He was just an old beach cowboy, who was in way over his head. John, whose real name was Charlie Neiman, rented rafts over here on Smathers Beach and sold joints to tourists. He was the guy expanding Angel's reach up north. This morning, they found John floating in Shark River up on the mainland."

"He either pissed off Angel or Angel's competition," said Alice. "Somebody may be trying to squeeze Angel out," she continued. "We know he flew into Miami with his bodyguard, Ezequiel Soto, the other day, but he flew back to Puerto Rico that same night alone. Soto was taken to the hospital for an apparent heart attack but was later released. The emergency room physician said he had a burn on his lower back consistent with a very powerful taser. We haven't found him. We suspect he's hiding in Miami."

Deputy Eubanks gave a thoughtful look for a moment. "Do you suppose somebody took out the bodyguard, grabbed Angel, scared the shit out of him, and let him go?"

"That's a possibility," answered Alice.

***

With his fuel tanks full, Orv checked to see that Leah was securely strapped into the right seat. He helped her adjust her headset, then fired up the motor. Ten minutes later, as they climbed out of Able Santamaria, Leah asked how long it would take to get to Key West.

"A little over two hours," said Orv replied over the intercom.

"I thought it was around a hundred miles," said Leah, sounding surprised.

"As the crow flies, it's about a hundred and forty miles from here. But your pilot has forged licenses and identification documents and is flying an illegally registered aircraft. Flying due north from Cuba to the Keys attracts a lot of attention. Flying in from the east, from the Bahamas, is much easier. We'll fly north-northeast to the Bahamas then turn and fly due west to the Keys."

Leah shrugged her shoulders and looked out at the beautiful tapestry passing below them. She remained silent for quite a while. After they had crossed the bay islands and were out over the strait, she turned to him. "Will you be returning to *Valle de Sagua*?"

Orv adjusted his microphone and sat up straight in his seat. "I don't want to overstay my welcome," he said honestly.

"I've decided that once my aunt and uncle are stable," she said while turning towards him, "I'm going to go back to California to divorce the bastard. That might take some time, I could use a reliable caretaker at the plantation. I need somebody who would watch over the place, make sure the staff is doing what they are supposed to be doing. We haven't had a good supervisor there for years."

Orv chuckled. "I'm a drug smuggler, wanted in the States, and not welcome in Cuba. I've got a horrible resume for the job."

"You're honest," said Leah. "I can find people who have glowing resumes, but I need somebody I can trust. It wouldn't be a difficult job. You simply watch over the staff, double check the accounting, and you can help Alejandro with his car projects from time to time. We even have a hangar on the property for this old relic."

He had to admit, it didn't sound like a bad gig. He needed a job, he needed a future. He might have just stumbled into something good. "I'll kick it around."

When the westernmost tip of the Bahamas, Williams Island, and Gold Cay came into view, Orv turned the plane due west to a compass heading of 270 degrees.

He was back on his normal commute, a route he knew very well. The weather was beautiful, the air was smooth, and the winds had calmed. A change in season seemed to be taking place.

As the Highway 1 bridge at Conch Key came into view, he turned a few degrees towards the south and crossed over the road at Marathon. Over Big Pine Key, he contacted Key West tower and stated his intent to land at the Garrison Bight Mooring Field. They gave him vectors to the southwest and asked him to notify the Coast Guard Station of his intentions.

Coast Guard Sector Key West alerted him of departing helicopter traffic as he started a big arching turn to the south near Fleming Key. He quickly spotted the orange and white Dolphin and determined that it would pass safely off his right side. He quietly hoped that it wouldn't circle behind him and follow him in to the bight.

The water in the narrow channel was smooth. The only boat in his way was a skiff, which darted to the left after noticing him. The man at the outboard waved as Orv passed. After setting down on the water, he looked for any unusual activity at the Coast Guard station, for any patrol boats ready to pounce on him. It appeared quiet; it looked like he had fooled them again.

Giles Boutier hurried out on the long dock when he saw Orv's plane taxiing towards his home. Orv spun the plane to face out, making it easier for Leah to climb out her side of the plane and making a sudden departure a little quicker. Orv didn't think he would have much of an opportunity to make a run for it; both the Navy and the Coast Guard had aircraft that were faster than his. Getting his plane away from the dock quickly wasn't going to make any real difference in his escape.

Giles secured the front line and hurried to the back after Orv almost perfectly nudged the plane up to the dock, killing the motor just before contact. Leah opened the door and climbed down the strut steps to the float.

Giles stood after securing the aft line and said loudly in his heavy French accent, "Orville, who is this beautiful creature that has dropped from your airplane?"

Orv exited the door and dropped down to the float. "Giles Boutier, I would like you to meet Leah Marchbanks."

Giles helped her step up onto the dock before he gently kissed her hand. "It is not often that an angel drops out of the heavens and steps onto my dock. Welcome to my home."

Leah giggled then turned to Orv. "Where did you find such a charming little man?"

Orv kneeled to double check the forward line that secured the plane to the dock. "He comes with the island. I think they've tried to send him back to where he came from, but he's like a bad penny."

Giles smiled at their comments then took Leah by the hand. "I am sure you have had a most harrowing flight. Please come rest by the pool and I will get you a drink."

Leah smiled. "Another time, my dear. My uncle is in the hospital and I need to get there right away."

"I am very sorry to hear that," said Giles. "I will take you to him myself. Is he at the Medical Center?"

Giles started to lead Leah towards his house and his car when she stopped. She turned and walked back to Orv. "Please don't wait for me. I know your being here presents a risk. I hope you'll fly back to the plantation and consider my offer." She stepped close, then got up on her tippy toes and kissed Orv on the cheek before she hurried off with the little Frenchman.

Orv stood on the dock and watched the two of them rush off while he considered his options. He had enough fuel to safely return to *Valle de Sagua* and really no other options at the moment. He didn't want to linger in Key West, he didn't want to attempt to refuel at the airport, and he didn't feel safe in the Bahamas. His options were limited.

He decided to return to the plantation and spend a few days considering Leah's offer of employment. Within the confines of the plantation, he was confident he would be safe. First, however, he needed something to eat. His small breakfast was wearing thin. He was starving. The closest place that he could think of that offered something decent to eat and a cold beer was the poolside Tiki Bar at the Fairfield Inn, about two blocks away. It wasn't the best place he could think of for lunch, but they served a pretty good burger and it was close. He double checked the aft line, locked the plane, then decided to walk rather than bike the short distance to the hotel.

***

Alice finished the breakout session that she facilitated then, after the break, stepped into a few of the other sessions to listen. She was proud of her staff. They were all doing a spectacular job. The day-long meeting was going far better than she had hoped. The locals seemed receptive to their ideas.

It was cold inside the hotel, however. She wished she had remembered to bring a sweater. Checking her watch, she saw she had almost forty minutes until the lunch session. The working lunch meeting, in the large conference room, was being hosted by the Coast Guard. They had several speakers slated to talk about coordination of efforts between local law enforcement and their efforts.

She shivered then decided to step outside to warm up for a few minutes. At the end of the long hallway, she could see sunshine, palm trees, and the shimmer of the sun off the pool. Perfect, she thought to herself. Ten minutes in the sun was just what she needed.

Orv had just finished his burger and a beer when he noticed a woman walk out of the hotel who reminded him of Alice. At first, he didn't believe it was her, but the way she walked, the way she moved, and her mannerisms convinced him. She walked to a chaise lounge near the pool's edge and sat down. He watched her for several minutes while his disbelief turned to shock. His Alice was sitting just twenty yards from him.

She looked good, he thought to himself. The years had been kind to her. It looked like she had a few gray hairs, but she wore them well. She had kept herself in shape, still slim and trim. He dropped a twenty and a ten on the bar and walked towards her, not sure what to say, not sure what her reaction would be after all those years. His mouth was dry, his hands were sweaty. He reminded himself to breathe. He couldn't believe how nervous he had become.

Approaching her from behind, he was still not a hundred percent convinced it was really his Alice. He figured he would start with a simple "hello" and see where it went from there. When he got to her chair, she looked up at him with indifferent and questioning eyes that seemed to look at a stranger.

He opened his mouth to say hello, but no words came out. Alice's face changed as she recognized him. Her eyes opened wide, he saw a hint of disbelief, then surprise. She suddenly sprang from her chair and threw her arms around his neck. His arms instinctively grabbed her around the small of the back, pulling her close.

Nothing had felt so good or so natural in over a decade. She held him tight but said nothing for several moments, her face buried into his chest. Their reunion was going much better than he had hoped when she released his neck, grabbed him by both arms, and suddenly said, "Oh my God, Orv, you can't be here. You have to leave!" The look on her face showed both panic and fear.

His heart sank as he saw her turn and glance towards the hotel door. "You're married?" he asked.

Her mind raced. She found herself in a place she had never been before. In her arms was the only man she had ever loved, a man she had shared so much with, a man with whom she desperately wanted to reconnect. She also held one of the criminals they were here to discuss. Inside the hotel sat twenty law enforcement officers who would love to collar the man she held. She found herself stuck in a strange place between love and duty.

"No," she blurted. "I'm with the DEA. Orv, I know what you've been doing." While she watched that sink in, she remembered her earlier conversation with Deputy Eubanks. "Oh my God!" she said while looking him in the eyes. He saw fear, almost a look of terror in her eyes. "You've got to run. Somebody got to Angel Moritz last night. They put his bodyguard in the hospital and beat him badly. His dealer, the guy they call John, was found dead in Shark River this morning. Somebody is dismantling Angel's business. They might come after you next."

While Orv was trying to comprehend everything that Alice had just told him, she added more. "There's an interagency drug enforcement meeting taking place inside. There are at least two dozen armed men and women in there who would love to get their hands on you! Orv, you need to run, you need to run away from here and don't look back!"

He still held her tightly by the hips, his eyes misted slightly. "Come with me," he said impulsively. "We'll fly away together, we'll make a new life somewhere. We can live on a beach where they'll never find us."

"I can't," she said weakly. "I can't go with you. I have a job, I have...I just can't."

Orv had no plan, no strategy, and no real thoughts. He knew he needed to get her away from the hotel, away from her fellow officers who would convince her to stay, the same people who wanted to take away his freedom. "Walk with me over to my plane. It's just a few minutes away. I have something I have to show you." He hoped she wouldn't ask what he wanted to show her; he hadn't made up that part of the lie yet.

"I can't," she protested while pointing towards the door. "I have meetings I need to get back to."

"You'll be back here in fifteen minutes, I promise."

She glanced at her watch. She had fifteen minutes to spare, and she couldn't be seen in the arms of a known drug smuggler. Then she remembered that nobody knew what Orv looked like. To them, he was known simply as an unidentified pilot. Just a figure hiding, a shadow that left footprints in the sand.

"Okay, fifteen minutes, but then you need to disappear forever. I can't be seen with you."

Before she had a chance to change her mind, he took her by the arm and led her out of the pool area into the parking lot and across Highway 1. As they walked briskly down Hilton Haven Road towards Giles' home on Trumbo Point, she looked at him. After all these years, he still had something about him that she found irresistible. She wanted so badly to hop in his plane and fly away to somewhere warm and sandy where they could live and love without all the stresses of the world. But she had duties and obligations. She had so much unfinished work she needed to complete, leaving with him wasn't possible.

She wondered how she could continue forward in her job knowing she had allowed a drug smuggler to escape.

When she opened the afternoon session, her speech was written to revolve around duty, principle, and honor. They were the words she had built her career around; they were words that had each lost their meaning to her in the last few minutes.

"I have so many things to say to you," she said as they walked briskly down the narrow street. "Since we only have a few minutes together, I'm going to say them quickly and bluntly. You can sort it out later."

Orv looked at her and smiled. "Okay, don't beat around the bush. Say what you need to say."

"First of all," she said softly while reaching for his hand. "I am so sorry I wasn't there for you after Jessica died. I know you were suffering too. I know you were dealing with the airline mess in Jamaica. Orv, I don't know what happened to me. I just shut down emotionally at a time when we desperately needed each other. Maybe if I could have dealt with things a little differently, we might have made it. I never blamed you for anything."

Orv started to say something before Alice shut him down. "Secondly, I am so pissed off at you right now. I know you've been flying drugs into the islands. I spend every waking minute of every day trying to stop people like you from ruining lives. To find out that you are involved in all this was a major slap in the face. How could you work for those people? How could you do something that makes it impossible for me to reconnect with you?"

Orv looked at her. He felt her warm, sweaty hand in his, he heard the love and the anger in her voice. In her anger, however, he heard an unmistakable passion. She still loved him, he still loved her. "I quit flying for Angel a while back," he said, slightly stretching the truth.

"That doesn't fix what you did," she said with a slightly elevated voice. "Why did you do something so stupid?"

He didn't have a real answer. He hadn't thought about it much. "I had to make money, and all I knew was flying. The FAA wasn't going to let me fly legally because they felt the need to punish me for some crazy scheme on some foreign island, so I found freight I could fly." Her only response was to squeeze his hand as hard as she could and give a frustrated grunt.

They turned off the narrow road into a condo parking lot and walked between two houses to a private pool and beach area. At the end of a long dock, she saw the familiar-looking plane with faded paint and the tail number N71WT. She laughed. The aircraft her cohorts were looking for was tied to a dock less than a thousand yards from where they were meeting.

Walking past the pool and out onto the dock, Orv released her hand and told her to stay put while he climbed the steps on the strut and unlocked the plane. As he crawled in the plane, Alice spotted the broken heart with her daughter's name painted on the side of the plane. She stepped onto the float and put her hand on the warm aluminum. It almost felt as if the heart was beating.

Orv climbed down from the plane and stood on the float facing her.

"This is a beautiful remembrance of an incredible soul," Alice said while looking toward Orv with a warm glow about her. The smile went away from her face when she saw his expression. His stance, his appearance, everything about him had changed. He looked determined, menacing, like he was a man on the edge of violence. "What did you want to show me?" she asked calmly.

"Alice, I need you to get in the plane," he said in a deep voice.

She didn't know exactly what his intentions were, but she wanted to be very clear with him at that moment. Falling back to her training, she spoke to him in a slow, deliberate, and commanding voice. "I need to get back to my meeting, and you need to leave Key West. I cannot protect you here."

He put his right hand behind his back, "Alice, I am sorry to do this. I am armed and desperate. You need to get in the plane. We'll figure this all out later, but for now, please do as I ask."

She smiled, uncertain if he was serious. She was slightly flattered that he would take such risks to get her back in his life. Taking a few steps towards him, she reached out and lightly laid her full hand on his chest. "I can't go with you," she said with a pained look on her face. "I have duties and obligations here that I can't leave. We have lots of pleasant memories, but that was so many years ago. Don't get me wrong; it's very tempting to climb into your plane and fly away with you, but I simply can't."

She put her arm around him and hugged him tightly. The little finger on her left hand felt the butt of the pistol he had tucked into the back of his shorts. Her instinct was to reach for the gun, pull it from his waistband, and drop it into the water while she had hold of him. Instead of trying for the gun, her hand reached up to the back of his head and gently pulled him to her. She kissed him, feeling his lips for the first time in over ten years. After a long, tender kiss, she released her hold on him.

Alice stepped back onto the dock, not knowing what his next move might be. He stood and silently looked at her. He looked deflated, his soul and his spirit seemed empty. She turned and walked away without looking back. He didn't say a word.

For the second time in his life, Orv watched Alice walk away, knowing he would probably never see her again. He had played his cards, he had hatched a stupid and impulsive plan to make her go with him, but it hadn't worked out, and he couldn't go through with actually threatening her with a weapon.

He watched as she walked the length of the dock, past the pool, then disappeared between the houses. She never looked back; from what he could see, she didn't seem to be crying or wiping her eyes. He imagined her leaving with a cold and stoic expression.

He climbed up the steps and crawled across the right seat into the plane. After turning on the master power switch, he hit the starter button and listened as the engine turned over. After ten turns of the prop, he released the button, primed the engine twice, then hit the button again. The old Beaver started on the first turn. Once he was convinced she was idling smoothly, he climbed back down to the float and untied both the forward and aft lines.

He took one more look at the space between the homes, the last place he had seen her. She hadn't stopped, she hadn't turned back. He crawled back up into the plane, settled into the left seat, and advanced the throttle.

Tears streamed down her face as she walked off the dock and past the pool. Between the houses, out of his sight, she stopped and used both hands to wipe the tears from her eyes and cheeks. When she heard the big radial engine start, her heart dropped. He wasn't chasing her; he was leaving.

A series of unfortunate events had dismantled their marriage ten years earlier. Now she was letting her duties as a law enforcement officer go ahead of her happiness. "My duties as a law enforcement officer," she said to herself as she realized that she was letting a job, not a religion, not a principle or a social-political belief, destroy her happiness. She remembered the nurse from the VA hospital, Nurse Gonzales. As Orv lay in the hospital in San Francisco, the nurse had told Alice, "If you want something, it's up to you to make it happen."

She turned and rushed back towards the pool. The plane was already moving away from the dock, but she had to try. Alice ran past the pool and out on to the dock. She yelled his name, knowing he wouldn't be able to hear her, but she had to try. At the end of the dock, she stopped and watched as he taxied away without her.

Orv slammed the palm of his hand down on the yoke. He had been stupid. He should have thought up a better plan. If he could have only gotten her to consider a different path for just a moment, just long enough to imagine a life together with him, she might have gone along. He let out a frustrated yell and punched the ceiling of the aircraft.

For a moment, he closed his eyes and asked himself, "Are you going to grouse over Alice or are you going to fly the plane?" He knew he couldn't do both, not safely. There would be plenty of time to drink himself into a self-pity-driven stupor once he got to Cuba, but for now, he needed to put her aside and fly the plane. He couldn't stay in these waters any longer. He opened his eyes with new clarity. Fly south and then drink a hundred thousand beers to forget some girl named Alice, he told himself.

At the channel, he turned ninety degrees to the left, towards the Garrison Bight mooring field. He checked his fuel and the oil pressure. He saw the oil temperature rising; everything looked good. No boats or helicopters stood in his way blocking his escape. Orv resisted the urge to turn and look back at the dock one last time. He knew it would be empty; she wouldn't be standing there. The image of the bare dock was one that would haunt him in his dreams. It was a picture he didn't need locked in his brain.

"Focus on the flight," he told himself again. Once in the air, he would turn south-southeast and follow the GPS directly to Isabela. Nobody focused on planes flying directly to Cuba. Planes flew over the little country every day on their way to the southern islands.

Orv buckled his waist belt then reached for his shoulder harness, just to make sure it was available if the flight got rough. The left side harness was twisted. He turned to fix it as the plane idled slowly down the channel. A movement out the window caught his eye. He knew better than to look, but before he could stop himself, his eyes glanced back at the dock. His mouth fell open, his breathing stopped, and his eyes widened. Alice was standing on the end of the dock, desperately waving her arms to him.

She knew she had missed her chance, but she had to try. Alice stood at the end of the dock and waved her arms fruitlessly over her head as the plane slowly taxied away from her down the channel. She yelled his name as loud as she could and looked for a passing boat that might pick her up and chase down the plane. She racked her brain, trying to think of anything to try to stop him, anything to get his attention, but he continued to slowly move away from her. It was painful to watch him leave, knowing that she had missed her chance. She wouldn't know where to start looking for him once his plane took off.

Alice waved, she screamed, she considered swimming after him; it wouldn't have worked, but it was something. She was about to give up, to return to the shore and live out her dreadful, dismal, loveless life alone when she saw the plane start a sharp turn in the channel.

CHAPTER TEN

"Have you seen Alice?" Johnny Reno asked Mark Young in the hallway.

Agent Young shook his head. "Not for an hour or so."

"She's supposed to start the next session, but nobody's seen her. I had a hotel maid check the restroom, and I've tried to call her cell phone. I'm not sure where she went," said Reno.

"That's weird," said Young. "I'll check by the pool and the little bar out there. Maybe she needed a cocktail after your last speech," he said with a laugh while slapping him on the shoulder.

Johnny Reno walked into the conference room and up to the front. "Sorry for the delay. We'll start this session in just a few minutes. Agent Weingarten got tied up in some unexpected business."

***

Orv shut down the motor as he approached the end of the dock. He didn't know why she had returned to the dock and waved him back, but he had his hopes. Sliding over to the right seat, he opened the door and stepped down onto the float. The plane's momentum glided him on a path that would take him past the end of the dock, missing it by about two feet.

Alice was flush, her hands shook. She reminded him of the girls in the old films, the high school girls about to meet Elvis or the Beatles. She was incredibly excited and nervous at the same time. "Take me with you!" she shouted as the plane glided towards the dock.

"Are you sure?" he asked.

"Yes!" she said. "I think," she followed weakly.

"You're going to have to jump!" he yelled to her.

She nodded, backed up, and waited until the float and Orv were passing as close as they would to the dock, then Alice took a few steps and jumped. Not wanting to end up in the water, she jumped a bit too far. Orv grabbed her and was knocked back against the plane, and her left shoe fell into the water. They laughed as he held her. She turned to watch her shoe drifting away behind the plane.

"I don't suppose there is any way to go back and get that?" she asked.

He smiled and kissed her. "I'll get you a new pair. We gotta go."

Crawling up into the plane, he restarted the motor and turned the plane around to resume the taxi out to the Garrison Bight channel. He helped her buckle in and adjust her headset.

"Can you hear me?" he asked over the intercom system.

"Yes," she replied. "Where are we going? I don't have any money, I don't have a passport, and I only have one shoe."

"You won't need money or a passport where we're going. I'll tell you about it after we're in the air. Hand me your cell phone."

She reached into the pocket of her blazer, retrieved her phone, and handed it to him. He opened his door and tossed it out.

"Hey, that's government property!" she said.

Orv smiled. "We wouldn't want to be accused of theft of government property. We'll leave it here for them."

Alice shook her head, wondering what she had gotten herself into. "Why does my microphone thingy smell like perfume?" she asked.

"My boss was wearing it about an hour ago," he said with a smile.

"Angel Moritz wears perfume?" she asked with a nervous laugh.

***

"I checked the parking lot," said Agent Young. "I talked with the front desk and the bartender out at the Tiki Bar; nobody's seen her. It's like she just disappeared."

Agent Reno looked at the floor. "The last time we were down here, she really freaked out thinking that she saw her ex-husband on the street corner." He thought about the strange episode for a moment then looked down the hallway. Pointing to a security camera at the end of the corridor, he said, "Let's see if we can spot her on the cameras in the last hour."

***

"Key West Tower, Beaver seven-one whiskey tango, ready for north water departure out of Garrison Bight channel," said Orv after pressing the comm button on the top of the yoke.

"Seventy-one whiskey tango, standby." Orv's heart skipped a beat when they asked him to standby. He was a wanted felon with a semi-kidnapped DEA agent aboard his illegally registered plane.

Fifteen long seconds later, the radio crackled. "Coast Guard Sector Key West, Beaver seven-one whiskey tango is departing Garrison Bight channel to the north. Do you still have an aircraft inbound?"

"Negative on the inbound, Key West. The channel is clear for your departing traffic."

"Seventy-one whiskey tango, clear for take-off. What is your destination?" said the friendly voice from Key West Tower.

"We're island hopping our way down to the U.S. Virgins. Can you give us vectors to the southeast? We're heading for Congo Town in the Bahamas."

She cocked her head sideways. What he said didn't make sense. "We're going to the U.S Virgins?"

Key West tower answered before he could acknowledge her. "Seventy-one whiskey tango, climb and maintain twenty-five hundred at three six zero. We'll give you vectors for Congo Town shortly."

Orv pushed the button again. "Twenty-five hundred and three six zero for seventy-one whiskey tango." He set the flaps for takeoff, took another look at the water ahead and the skies around him, then advanced the throttle. "No," he said while turning the rudder left against the plane's desire to follow the engine's torque to the right. "We're not going to the Virgin Islands."

***

In a little room tucked behind the hotel's front desk, Agents Reno and Young reviewed the video tapes. Since they were only looking back an hour, and there were only eight cameras, it took them just a matter of minutes to find her image captured on the hallway camera. She walked alone down the hall towards the pool and outdoor bar. The only thing out of the ordinary they could see was that she walked with her arms crossed. She seemed to be cold.

Moving to the pool camera, they saw her walk out and sit down on a chaise lounge chair in the sun alone. They watched a man approached her from behind. She stood and put her arms around his neck and hugged him as he put his arms around her waist. They obviously knew each other.

"Is that the ex-husband?" asked Young.

"That would be my guess. I didn't get a look at him when we were here before," answered Agent Reno.

They continued watching. Agent Weingarten and the man spoke for a short time, then he pointed to his left and they walked out of the pool area together. She seemed to go willingly. According to the time stamp on the video, the meeting and exchange had happened only twenty-two minutes earlier.

Agent Young looked at his watch then turned to Reno. "Why don't you check the rest of these to see if she appears on any video after they walk out. I'll go out and follow the direction they walked from the pool and see if I can find any evidence in the parking lot or beyond."

Out at the pool, Young searched in the direction that his boss and the unidentified man had walked in the video. He was retracing the steps he had taken during his first search, but now he looked for clues rather than for Alice. Did she drop anything, did she leave any clues for them to find if she was leaving under duress?

After a quick search of the walkway and the parking lot with his head down, looking for clues on the ground, he stopped and looked around. They must have left in a car, he assumed. They might have walked away, but there wasn't much in the area except for a couple of fast food restaurants and a small neighborhood across the street. He walked south on Highway 1. It seemed the likely direction they might have gone if on foot, towards town.

***

As Orv pulled the yoke back towards his chest, Alice watched him doing what he loved to do, fly. A wild range of emotions overtook her as they lifted off the water. She was thrilled at the prospect of the adventure ahead of her, but she was also scared to death of the unknown. She wondered how she could unwind the rash decisions she had made over the last half hour if she changed her mind.

They might believe a concocted story that she took advantage of a sudden opportunity to infiltrate the drug ring, although it seemed like a stretch since she flew away with her ex-husband. She might try to tell the truth, but that didn't seem like a very good argument as she imagined herself on her supervisor's side of the desk.

Realizing that her actions and decisions over the past thirty minutes were probably life changing, Alice chose to ignore her problems for the moment. She turned and looked at Orv as he coaxed the old plane into the air. He glanced at her with that smile she had fallen in love with a million years earlier. She wanted to unbuckle and crawl into his lap and to become completely absorbed by him, but that would have to wait for later.

Key West tower directed them to turn due east and climb to five thousand feet after a few minutes.

"Where are we going?" Alice asked after the turn.

"North Central Cuba," Orv replied with the same vocal inflection he would have used if he told her they were going to Cleveland.

Alice was surprised, a bit shocked, and suddenly very anxious about her rash choice to go with him. She conjured up images of landing at a heavily guarded compound owned by a slick drug lord named something like Pablo Chacon. Then she remembered that very few drugs were produced in Cuba. The country did a really good job of drug interdiction.

"Cuba?" she finally responded after almost a full minute.

"Yeah, I've been offered a job managing a plantation near the little town of Isabela de Sagua."

"What do they grow on the planation?" she asked, trying to be cautious.

Orv looked over at her and smiled. "Sugar cane, bananas, and some of the best vegetables I have ever eaten. Did you think I was taking you to a marijuana farm?"

She was a little embarrassed for asking the question but tried not to show it. "I'm just curious. I didn't know you knew anything about managing a plantation."

As he leveled the plane at five thousand feet, he gave her a funny look. "I don't, but Leah, the owner, seems to like me. She thinks I'm trustworthy."

"Leah?" asked Alice in a strange tone.

***

Johnny Reno walked to the head of the conference room that was filled with law enforcement officers. "Ladies and gentlemen, sorry for the delay. We have a situation; Agent Weingarten is missing." They had grown impatient and even a bit angry at the lack of information and the delay in starting the next session. When Agent Reno announced one of their own was missing, every head in the room snapped around and became instantly engaged.

"Security video shows Agent Weingarten speaking to and hugging a man near the pool about thirty-five minutes ago. After talking for a short period of time, the man pointed towards the parking lot and they both left the area. She seemed to leave willingly, but she doesn't answer her cell phone, which is out of character, and it is completely unlike her to miss this session."

Sheriff Gothberg spoke up first. "Do you have any other information? A general description of the man or the type of car they might have left in? Have you searched the hotel building?"

"Is there any reason for concern at this point?" asked Deputy Eubanks. "Is there any information you have that might lead you to believe she is in danger?"

Johnny Reno looked up at the ceiling for a moment while his mind went through every bit of information he could remember that might be helpful. "When we were down here last week, Agent Weingarten thought she saw her ex-husband on the street corner as we were driving. She became very emotional and even jumped out of the car before I could get it stopped. The ex-husband's name is Orville Hendricks. I tried to find information on him, at her request, but he has either died or become a ghost. No address, no driver's license, no hits with the IRS, and no valid pilot's license."

"Pilot's license?" asked Key West Police Chief Don Brewer.

"Yeah," replied Agent Young. "Her ex was a commercial pilot years ago, but the FAA had pulled his license after some bad business deal in Jamaica."

Both Reno and Young knew of Alice's suspicions that her ex, Orville Hendricks, might be the pilot of the Beaver, the plane suspected of carrying drugs into the islands. They also knew, as they shot a glance at each other, that revealing that information could ruin her career.

Chief Brewer noticed the glance between the two agents. "What else aren't you telling us?"

Johnny Reno let out a long sigh. "Agent Weingarten suspected that her ex-husband might be the pilot of an aircraft that may be connected to Angel Moritz."

"What information do you have on that plane?" asked Brewer.

"It's a de Havilland Beaver float plane," said Young. He flipped through his notebook until he found the tail number. "November seven-one whiskey tango."

It didn't take long for the officers in the room to start putting together scenarios. Chief Brewer started handing out tasks. "Agents Reno and Young, I want you to go with housekeeping and search every occupied room in this hotel. If nobody answers, go in and look. If the hotel gives you any shit about warrants, tell them we need to see all the immigration papers on every employee." Turning to Sheriff Gothberg, he said, "Cal, will you put out an APB on Agent Weingarten and the man she met at the pool?"

Coast Guard Lieutenant Commander Tim Lalley stepped forward while holding his cell phone to his ear. "Key West Tower says a floatplane, a Beaver, seventy-one whiskey tango, took off from Garrison Bight channel within the last half hour, heading for Congo Town, Bahamas for fuel then on to the USVI."

"How far is the Bahamas from here?" asked Agent Young.

Lalley thought for a moment. "Two hundred and fifty, maybe three hundred miles."

"What speed does a Beaver fly, two hundred knots or so?" asked Brewer.

Lalley laughed, his phone still held to his ear. "We still operate a few Beavers up in Alaska. With floats, and a really strong tailwind, they might do one fifty."

"So the plane could be a hundred miles away?" said Agent Reno.

Lalley held up his pointer finger then turned away from the group and spoke into his phone. "Thank you," he said after a moment. "Keep me posted."

Turning back to the group, he dropped his cell phone into his pocket before saying, "Key West tower has lost contact with the Beaver. Their transponder is no longer transmitting, meaning they've turned it off. The plan has either landed, crashed, or they are trying to be invisible. The Navy's launching two F5 Tigers to chase them down."

"How long will that take?" asked Sheriff Gothberg.

Lalley tilted his head slightly to the left then right. "If they are airborne in the next ten minutes, at five hundred miles an hour, they should have a visual on them in twenty-five minutes, assuming they are still out there."

***

"How long did you fly for Angel Moritz?" Alice asked as they plowed through the sky.

"A little over five years," Orv answered honestly with no hint of guilt.

Remembering the flow of money, from Moritz to Orv to the Cystic Fibrosis Foundation, she played coy with him. "You must have put away a lot of money," she said.

Orv shook his head then looked at her. "Operating an old plane, living the lifestyle; it's all very expensive. I don't have much besides this beat-up old bucket and the clothes on my back. Actually, these clothes were recently given to me."

She had always known that Orv was a horrible liar the few times he had tried. She was fairly certain he wasn't lying to her now. "How much money did you give to Cystic Fibrosis over the last five years?"

His head jerked towards her, surprised that she knew. He quietly answered, "As much as I could, all of it."

She saw a tear form in the corner of his eye behind the temple piece of his Maui Jim sunglasses. She gently put her hand on his arm. Until that moment, she didn't understand how profoundly Jessica's death had affected him. Alice had questioned the sanity of her decisions over the last hour. Suddenly, she felt she was right where she needed to be, right where she was supposed to be at that moment in her life.

"Tell me about Cuba, about the plantation," she said, hoping to change the subject.

Orv sniffed slightly, then wiped the tear from his eye. "I don't know if you remember, but fifteen years ago, when I was flying freight for the Flying Tigers, we broke down in Cuba for two days."

Alice smiled. "Yeah, now that you say that, I remember."

"While we waited for parts, I borrowed a motorcycle and found the most amazing little town, out on a peninsula on the north coast. A little piece of paradise protected by a group of bay islands. The town is nicknamed the Venice of Cuba, a place known to the locals as Isabela."

"It sounds wonderful," she said.

"An American family has owned and operated a plantation just up the river from the town for seventy or eighty years. Leah, the owner, needs to return to California and has asked me to manage the place for her."

"Don't I need a passport to get into Cuba?" asked Alice.

Orv stared out the window for a moment or two. "Leah's family seems to have some favored nation status with the Castro regime. I was surrounded by Cuban

Customs when I landed at the airport inland from her plantation. I thought, with a fake passport, a fake pilot's license, and no entry visa, that I was probably going to prison for a few years. Leah came driving up and everybody backed down. They let me go just because I was with her. I think we'll be fine if we stay in the general area of Isabela."

***

A hundred and seventy miles behind Orv and Alice, while a fruitless search of the hotel and surrounding area took place, two Navy F-5N Tigers roared out of Naval Air Station Key West and turned east. They accelerated to Mach .9; six hundred and eighty-five miles an hour, while climbing to twenty thousand feet. Two and a half minutes out of Key West, their AN/APQ-159 radar systems acquired a slow-moving aircraft flying east towards the Bahamas. The onboard tactical computer calculated it would take the Tigers twelve minutes to intercept their target.

***

A sense of disbelief swept over Orv every time he glanced over at the woman next to him. An hour and a half earlier, as he ate his burger at the hotel Tiki Bar, he was convinced he would never see her again. Now she was sitting in his right seat, flying with him to a new life together. It was all too good to be true, but he knew he wasn't dreaming. Of all the crazy thoughts rolling around in his head, the one that boiled to the top was sleep. He wondered if Alice sleeping next to him would change or eliminate his nightmares.

Orv scanned his instrument panel for the second time in the last minute. His fuel was fine, the oil pressure and temp were normal, his manifold pressure looked good. He listened to the engine; it was running normal and smooth. He was on course, the plane was trimmed properly.

It was almost flying itself, maintaining heading and altitude with very little adjustment from him. But something seemed off; he just couldn't put his finger on it.

"About another thirty minutes," he said to Alice with a smile. He wanted her to feel comfortable, even though he didn't. "You're going to love this place."

"Is there a beach nearby?" she asked while putting her hand on his shoulder.

"Beautiful beaches, miles and miles of them, and not a soul in sight," he replied.

He scanned the instrument panel a third time, he double checked his GPS heading on the compass, he listened to the engine and then paid attention to the vibrations he felt through his body. Everything was normal. He told himself to relax and start thinking about the landing. It had been more than ten years since he had landed on a grass field. There was no centerline, no glideslope aids; just him and the dirt. He wished he had walked the strip once when he had the chance. Was it firm and smooth, were the cows out on the runway? He rolled his eyes. What was he worried about? It was a piece of cake compared to landing ahead of a thunderstorm on water.

Assuming the strip was clear, putting the Beaver down on the long field should be easy. But he couldn't shake that feeling that something was amiss.

***

The flight of two Navy Tigers led by veteran training pilot, Captain Mike Giltzow, call sign "Guitar," slowed to three hundred knots and started a descent to seventy-five hundred feet as they closed on the slow-moving aircraft ahead and below them. Forty feet to his right was his trainee, Lieutenant Junior Grade Denise Smith, call sign "DeeDee."

Captain Giltzow liked the kid. He saw potential in her abilities as an aviator and an officer. He liked her decision-making process, and having only flown with her a few times, had grown to trust her.

"Our bogie is fifteen miles at five thousand," said Guitar. "He should be right below the cloud cover. I'll hang back and stay high while you make visual ID and contact. Have you done this before?"

"Only in training," DeeDee answered. "A couple of times on the simulator."

"Okay," said Guitar. "After you ID our target, go in on his port side keeping about two hundred yards separation and make both visual and radio contact. Remember, aircraft seem to be magnetically attracted to each other up here; they naturally want to bump into each other. Your aircraft wants to go where you're looking. Don't close to less than two hundred."

"Roger that," replied DeeDee.

The mission was to make contact with the pilot and instruct them to land at the nearest strip. The information given after they had scrambled out of Key West was the plane had a possible kidnapping victim aboard. DeeDee figured it was a father trying to take his child from his estranged wife or something mild. The Navy had no reason to provide the pilots with information that the plane was suspected of transporting drugs and now potentially held a kidnapped federal agent.

Watching her radar, DeeDee descended into the bank of clouds but made sure to stay behind and well to the left of her target. She slowed to two hundred knots just before she broke out of the clouds at fifty-eight hundred feet. The target was three miles ahead and just below her. On the horizon, she could see the western coastline of the Bahamas.

DeeDee was only vaguely familiar with the de Havilland Beaver, but she knew immediately that the aircraft she was approaching wasn't the plane they were after. "Guitar, verify our target is a float plane." She increased her speed to close on the small plane.

"Roger, the Beaver is a high-winged, single-prop aircraft with two large floats," replied Guitar.

"I'm seeing a low-wing, bubble-cockpit crop duster," said DeeDee.

Guitar cussed. "Stand by; I'm coming down for a look." He verified the radar location of both aircraft ahead of him and pushed his nose down towards the clouds. Breaking out into the open, he saw DeeDee off his portside and the small plane ahead and below him. He closed to within three hundred feet but stayed just above and to the right of the target aircraft. Having grown up on a farm in Iowa, he was very familiar with the yellow plane below.

"Key West, Guitar flight of two. We have a visual on the bogie you assigned to us. We have intercepted an Air Tractor, AT-802, negative on the Beaver."

CHAPTER ELEVEN

For twenty minutes, Cuba's northern bay islands had been off their right side. At Cayo del Cristo, Orv turned south and flew the entire length of Cayo de la Cruz in just minutes. He pointed to a little peninsula that jutted out from the mainland. "That's Isabela de Sagua. To the left is the mouth of the Sagua la Grande river, and a few miles up the river is a little plantation called *Valle de Sagua*. We'll land on a grass strip on the plantation."

She nodded as he began his descent.

***

"How could they mistake a Beaver floatplane for a crop duster?" asked Agent Reno in a frustrated voice.

"The Navy identified three possible targets, slow moving and flying low," said Coast Guard Lieutenant Commander Lalley. "One they were able to identify one by transponder and radio, one was on a heading towards Cuba, and the third was moving east towards the Bahamas. The Beaver pilot told ATC they were going to the Bahamas, so the Navy went after that target."

"What happened to the other target, the one heading towards Cuba?" asked Reno.

"They're looking for it," said Lalley. "Cuba requires a degree of caution when it comes to our military. The Navy has diverted a P-8 Poseidon to try to reacquire the southern target."

The search of the hotel and the surrounding area had yielded nothing. An all-points bulletin had been broadcast, and a roadblock had been set up on the eastern end of Big Coppitt Key.

Agent Mark Young stood up in the back of the room. He raised his right hand while his left hand held his cell phone. "I've got her cell phone tracking," he said loudly over the conversation in the room. Everybody stopped talking. "The last three locations the service provider recorded were here at the hotel, then a spot about eighteen hundred feet west of the hotel. The last one was about a thousand feet north of that, now an hour and forty-seven minutes ago. They've had no location since that."

While most eyes turned towards the map of the area that had been pinned to the wall, Chief Brewer turned to Sheriff Gothberg and Agent Young and said, "Let's take a walk down to the end of Trumbo Point."

Stepping out of the hotel into the heat and humidity of the day, the three crossed the highway and started down the narrow road, not knowing they were retracing Alice's last steps on American soil. Gothberg radioed dispatch, instructing them to place a car at the eastern end of Hilton Haven Road to check any cars leaving the little area. They walked slowly, methodically, looking for any clues.

The crowded little peninsula that jutted out from the island held about twenty homes and three small condominium buildings. Searching every home and boat along the road would take a lot of time and resources. But Brewer focused on the last location, a thousand feet north of Trumbo Point. He knew from many previous searches that the information was sketchy at best; cell phone signals often played tricks, sometimes showing them miles from their actual location.

Near the end of Hilton Haven Road, they spoke with an elderly man who was walking a small poodle. They asked him if he had seen a man and a nicely dressed woman in their mid-fifties walking around in the last few hours. He said he hadn't. When they asked if he had seen a seaplane at any of the docks in the area, the man provided a wealth of information.

"Yeah, that old plane comes in from time to time and ties up to Giles Boutier's dock. It says "Tarpon Jim Fishing Charters" on the side, but I don't remember that Red ever had a plane." The old man laughed. "I think it's a cover for whatever he's really doing."

"Was the plane here this morning?" asked Chief Brewer.

"Yeah," replied the man. "It left out of here an hour or two ago. I didn't see it go, but I heard it, noisy son-of-a-bitch. Rosie barks and barks every time that plane comes or goes; something about that old engine that gets her going."

"Can you point out which home is Giles Boutier?" asked Sheriff Gothberg.

"No need," said Chief Brewer as he gestured towards the north. "I know Giles. Let's go see if he's home."

They thanked the elderly man for his time. Agent Young got a growl and a snarl when he bent to try to pet Rosie. After the men laughed at Rosie's antics, they followed the Chief towards a home at the end of the point.

Giles' home sat on a very expensive piece of real estate. It was the last home on Trumbo Point, which afforded the north side of the house and the pool with some amazing views. The home, built in the early seventies, had been updated many times. Giles, a French citizen, had owned it for the last six years.

After knocking on the door and receiving no answer, Brewer led the men around to the north side of the home, where he saw the short, stout Frenchman working on a boat out on the dock. Rounding the inviting-looking pool, they stepped out on to the long dock.

"Giles," yelled Brewer while waving.

"Donny!" answered the man on the boat after looking up. "What a surprise to see you here."

The boat Boutier worked on was an impressive 12.6-meter racing catamaran. Young, a weekend sailor recognized the sleek SL-33 One Design immediately. It was a boat built for only one reason, to go fast.

"Are you here to take my new baby out for a sail?" asked Giles in his heavy accent as he stepped onto the dock to greet the men.

"Maybe another day," said Brewer. "This is Sheriff Gothberg with Monroe County, and this is Agent Young with the DEA. Gentlemen, Giles Boutier," said Brewer before they all shook hands.

"It is an honor to meet you," said Giles. "May I get you something cool to drink in the shade by the pool?"

Brewer smiled. "No thank you, Giles, perhaps another time. We are looking for a woman that may have come out this way. A taller woman, slender, well dressed, mid-fifties. She was probably with a man wearing tan shorts and a Bahama-style shirt, also in his mid-fifties."

"I haven't seen any women like that today," said Giles. "The man, wearing shorts and a Bahama style shirt? That is half the men on this island."

"How about a seaplane?" asked the Sheriff. "We heard there was a seaplane at your dock this morning."

"Yes," replied Giles with a smile. "My friend, Orville. He came this morning with a beautiful woman. I took the woman to the hospital to see her sick uncle. When I got back, Orville had left."

Young perked up. "Was the plane an orange and white de Havilland Beaver?"

"Yes," said Giles. "Orville occasionally uses my dock when he comes to the island."

"Where is Orville from?" asked Brewer.

"He is from Miami."

"Does he come down here often?" asked Brewer.

"I have not seen him in a very long time, but he came last week and was on the island for a night or two. Then he came again this morning, but as you can see, it looks like he has left again."

"He arrived with a woman?" inquired Young.

Giles smiled. "Yes, a beautiful, charming creature. Her name is Leah, from San Clemente, California. Her aunt and uncle live here part of the year, but unfortunately, her uncle suffered a mild heart attack yesterday. Orville was kind enough to bring the lovely woman to my dock. I drove her to the hospital just a few hours ago."

"You weren't here when the plane left?" asked Young.

"No," replied Giles. "Do you think my friend Orville left with your tall, slender woman?" asked Giles with a smile. "Those pilots! He comes in with one beautiful woman and leaves with another. Oh, to be a pilot."

Sheriff Gothberg wasn't charmed by Giles. "What does Orville have in his plane when he arrives at your dock?"

"What do you mean?" asked Giles. "He always comes only by himself, until today. He has nothing on the plane except himself and a small backpack."

"Do you know why he comes down here? Does he have business here?" inquired Gothberg.

Giles had heard things over the years, but he had cast off the rumors. Even if they were true, he didn't care. Orville was his friend. "I don't know why he comes here. I am only happy that he visits me from time to time."

"You said the woman's name was Leah?" asked Gothberg. "Is she still at the hospital?"

"I don't know," replied Giles truthfully. "That is where I left her."

They thanked Giles for his time. Brewer called for a car to meet them and take them to the Key West Medical Center. Finding Leah was very easy in the small hospital. She said she was happy to meet with the three investigators.

Sitting in a waiting room, they introduced themselves. "We understand you flew in on a seaplane this morning," said Chief Brewer.

"Yes," said Leah with a smile. "It's the only way to get here," she gushed. "Such a beautiful and quick flight too."

"Where did you come from this morning?" he inquired.

"Miami," said Leah without a pause.

"You flew here with a man named Orville Hendricks?"

"Hendricks?" said Leah. "Is that his last name? I only know him by his first name. He introduced himself to me as Orv."

When asked, Leah told them she was separated from her husband in California and currently living in a condo owned by her family in Miami. She had met Orv the day before at little bar named Freddie's, a block from her condo. According to Leah, they were having a drink together when she got the news of her uncle's heart attack.

Orv offered to fly her to Key West and she took him up on it.

Leah was able to provide them the address of the condo that her family actually owned, the location of the bar. She even described the marina where she met the pilot that morning. She was so believable and answered their questions so quickly and completely that when they ran out of questions, they were convinced she was being completely truthful.

"Do you know where he was going after bringing you here?" asked Sheriff Gothberg.

"He didn't say," she answered.

"Did he mention the Bahamas or Cuba to you?"

"He did not," she replied.

They thanked her and started to leave when Agent Young turned back towards her. "Missus Marchbanks, you didn't ask us why we were questioning you about the pilot."

"Of course, I'm curious," she said with a smile. "You suspect him of a crime, a serious crime given he is being investigated by the Chief of Police, the Sheriff, and the DEA. But even if I inquired, you wouldn't give me any details. It seems like a waste of breath to ask the question."

The three men left the hospital convinced they had been told the truth.

***

Finding the plantation and the runway proved as easy as Orv had described to Alice. He followed the river inland a few miles then spotted the house with the big veranda and colorful umbrellas. He spotted the buildings to the east of the home, and the hangar at the end of the grass strip. The old orange windsock indicated a wind from the west, Orv circled south of the plantation and lined up on the field.

After lowering the float wheels, he double checked the flap settings, scanned the instrument panel again, and glanced at the windsock adjacent the hangar. He set the plane down a quarter of the way down the strip, still giving him more than enough room to gently stop. At the end of the strip, he spun her around a hundred and eighty degrees and taxied back towards the hangar.

Glancing over at his passenger as he shut down the engine, his shock began to take hold. He was sitting in his plane, on a private plantation in Cuba, with his Alice sitting in the seat next to him. For the last two hours, he had been focused on the flight. He had quelled his emotions and focused on the task at hand. Orv could feel the excitement, the passion, and a hundred other thoughts and feelings coming to the surface. He felt as if something mighty had taken a right-hand turn into his world. He fought back tears while he desperately tried to find his words. His mouth became dry, his hands shook.

Alice removed her headset and hung it on the yoke in front of her. She turned to say something to Orv but stopped. The look on his face surprised her. She saw a mix of confusion, fear, and love. It was a tender look mixed with a slight bit of anxiety. She understood; a few hours earlier, she had been standing on stable ground, leading a conference in a hotel with twenty people listening to her speak. A few hours earlier, she had been a DEA department lead with a staff of fourteen, a pension, a small condo, and an uncomfortably high car payment. In a matter of two hours, she had thrown it all away and leapt onto the float of a passing airplane.

She herself felt love and confusion and more than a bit of fear. Alice reached out for Orv and held him tightly as their raw emotions swept over them.

***

The Navy P-8 Poseidon was a modified version of the Boeing 737-800ERX designed to conduct anti-submarine warfare, anti-shipping warfare, and shipping interdiction. Equipped with the powerful Raytheon APY-10 multi-mission surface search radar, the NAS Jacksonville-based aircraft had the ability to look far beyond the horizon.

Aboard the P-8, just aft of the flight deck, five operators monitored multi-function displays that could be configured to display whatever sensors that were most important under the current circumstances. Given the simplicity of the search NAS Key West was requesting, Commander Rob Hill assigned only one operator, Petty Officer Michele Watson, to the task while the remaining four operators continued with the training mission.

While the P-8 had orbited thirty-thousand feet above the Gulf of Mexico, nearly four hundred miles northwest of Isabela, with everybody aboard concentrating on the training mission at hand, the powerful onboard Fox-88 tactical computer had quietly recorded every radar image within its range. Petty Officer Watson simply directed the "88" to replay the radar images from sector Key West for the last two hours in high speed. In a matter of minutes, she was isolating and dismissing aircraft flight paths that didn't line up with the missing aircraft. It took her less than ten minutes to find and dismiss the Tiger's crop duster and then to identify the second slow-moving aircraft.

Watson was unable to determine exactly where the aircraft landed but narrowed it to a small area on the island's central southern coast. She forwarded the information to NAS Key West and went back to her training duties.

Orv wiped his eyes then wiped the tears from Alice's face. He nodded his head towards Alejandro, who had appeared in front of the plane with a small aircraft tug. Orv sniffed. "This guy's amazing. I'll bet that tug has been completely restored."

After climbing down from the plane and quick introductions, Orv and Alejandro carefully moved the Beaver into the hangar, watching to see that the vertical stabilizer cleared the top of the door. Orv thanked him for the help and started towards the main house, gesturing to Alice which way to go. As he left the hangar, he looked over his shoulder and saw the mechanic up on the starboard float wiping oil from the engine cowling. Orv shook his head and resisted the urge to turn back to help.

As they walked towards the house, Orv pointed out the shop and told Alice that they would come back later to see the cars. He told her about the size of the plantation, the crops grown, and the family's history on the island. "That's crazy," said Alice upon hearing the story of the American family flying under the radar of the sixty-year embargo against Cuba. Her curiosity and investigational background wanted to look further into the story, but she reminded herself that she didn't work in the American justice system any longer. Orv gestured towards the right and up the hill.

Passing the workers' small homes, they saw several people sitting out on the porches who suspiciously waved to Orv and the tall woman who accompanied him. Speculation and gossip had swirled when the American stranger had suddenly appeared. The staff wondered if he was a new romantic interest of Leah. But now, on the day their employer had returned to the United States, the stranger reappeared and walked hand in hand with another woman. The employees of the plantation had enough conversational fodder and conjecture to keep them busy for weeks.

Orv and Alice walked to the main house and up the grand stairs that led to the entry. Maria greeted them inside the front door and motioned the two towards the veranda. She had been directed by Leah to treat Orv like an honored guest should he return to the plantation. She wasn't sure how she was supposed to treat the woman who had shown up with him.

"Oh my gosh, Orv, it's so beautiful here," said Alice as they walked out on to the veranda that overlooked the river valley and the lush green crops that grew below.

"It's quite a place," he replied. "I think I could live here if I had to. Have a seat. I'll see if I can find a couple of mojitos and some appetizers."

***

Four hours after Orv's Beaver lifted off from Garrison Bight, a Gulfstream G550 took off from the Homestead Air Reserve Base in Southern Florida and turned south towards Jamaica. From the exterior, N388AG looked like any other $45-million-dollar business jet, with the exception of a small pod mounted under the center of the fuselage and a smaller dome that bulged out the top. Inside, the usually luxurious jet was instead crammed full of electronics. Three operators sat aft of the cockpit monitoring panels that were fed information by a series of highly sensitive cameras, a sophisticated AESA radar system, and magnetic anomaly detection equipment.

Cuban air traffic controllers were so used to hearing 388AG's call sign flying over the island that they had quit questioning the seemingly spontaneous flight plans. By flying from different airports along the southern and eastern coastlines of in the States, the Gulfstream could fly over various parts of Cuba as needed to conduct its surveillance without raising suspicions. The Cuban controllers figured the plane was the toy of some rich American businessman who liked the money in the U.S. and the women in Jamaica.

388AG's current mission was to fly over the Villa Clara Province and conduct a search for a de Havilland Beaver that was tracked to the area but lost from radar as it descended. Crossing this island at thirty thousand feet, the operators were able to image and analyze a wide swath of the region. The onboard tactical computer highlighted objects of interest on the ground, specifically shapes and profiles that could be a Beaver floatplane.

As the Gulfstream descended into Norman Manley International Airport off Kingston, Jamaica, an operator on board sent a flash message to 69th Reconnaissance Group at Grand Forks Airforce Base in North Dakota that included millions of bytes of data to be further analyzed and investigated. Within an hour, four aircraft and three other suspicious objects near airstrips or large bodies of water had been identified. The information was sent via secure email to a contact on the ground in Cuba for visual observation.

***

The years melted away as Alice and Orv sat on the veranda and talked. After enjoying cocktails and appetizers, then a delicious dinner prepared by Maria, they moved to some more comfortable chairs that faced the west, so they could watch the sunset over the Cuban countryside. Alice laughed and smiled as they spoke. Orv had never felt so happy. While telling him the story about her leaping from the car when she saw him in Key West, he placed his hand on hers as it lay on the armrest of her chair. She smiled.

Maria approached them with a younger female staff member in tow. The two staffers seemed uncomfortable as they asked, using hand signals and pointing, if the American couple required one or two bedrooms for the night. Alice smiled when she understood what they were asking. She blushed then held up just one finger.

***

After a long day of hospitals and doctors and being questioned by the police and the DEA, Leah drove her aunt home to her condo. After making certain that the elderly woman was settled and comfortable, Leah sat out on the deck and called her father to report her uncle's condition.

Jack Brown, Leah's father, had become too old and frail to travel. His mind was sharp, but his body was slowly failing him.

"Hi, Dad," said Leah when her father answered the phone.

"How's Teddy?" he asked.

"He's doing well. They say it was a minor heart attack. He'll stay in the hospital another day or two, then he can go home. Aunt Maggie is hanging in there. We're back at their condo. She's resting. I recommended that they consider heading back to San Clemente after he's stable. You have better medical facilities out there to help him recover."

Leah heard a sigh on the other end of the line. "I'm glad you were back there and able to help out. How are you doing?" asked her father.

"I'm fine," said Leah. "I've decided to come home and file for divorce from Doug. He'll turn it into a long and nasty process, but I have to do it."

"It might not be as long or as nasty as you think," said her father.

From his tone she could tell he was up to something. "Why is that?" she asked.

"A few years ago, Doug told me about a new technology his company was working on. It sounded very promising, so I bought some stock in the company through one of our corporations. I told some of the guys down at the club about it and they bought some too. Over the years, my friends and our family corporations have continued to buy stock in Chamberlin Medical. Between my buddies, and four or five of our corporations, we own controlling interest. Numb nuts has been so busy chasing skirt that he never noticed who owned what stock." Her father laughed. "It's time for the stockholders to take over and replace both the board and the president of the company."

Leah frowned. "You can't fire him because I'm divorcing him," she said.

"No," said Jack Brown. "That would be wrong. But we can fire him and start a legal investigation because he has been misappropriating company funds."

"What?" she asked.

"The millions of dollars he has been investing into research and development has been paid to another company, an R&D firm called Eldec, or something like that. It turns out that the company is a shell. They don't exist except for on paper. They are wholly owned by just a few shareholders, Douglas Marchbanks and his drinking buddies." Leah's mouth fell open. She knew her husband was a snake, but she didn't know he was a thief.

"You come home and file for divorce," said her father. "I'm going to call a shareholders' meeting, elect a new board, fire Doug, then ask the District Attorney and the Securities and Exchange Commission to start an investigation into all of them. He's going to have a hard time contesting your divorce from prison."

Leah smiled and shook her head. The current board of directors was made up of Doug's golf and college buddies. She knew they were very well paid and that the company spent tremendous amounts of money going on very expensive corporate retreats. The coup her father suggested would turn the town upside down.

***

In an office complex in North Miami, Tom Eason gathered his confidants, the group he had come to think of as his "board of directors." The events of the previous evening had gone both very well and disastrously wrong. The kidnapping of Angel Moritz in the middle of a large crowd gathered at the taxi stand at Miami International had been flawless. His bodyguard went down like a ton of bricks while his two men ushered Moritz into a waiting SUV as the crowd looked at the big man convulsing on the ground. In a nearby warehouse, they "convinced" the cocky Puerto Rican that his business dealings in the State of Florida were done. The orders had been "Don't make him bleed, but make it hurt real bad." Eason was pretty sure they would never see Angel Moritz again.

Unfortunately, on the west coast of the state, things had gone horribly wrong. The two men Eason had asked to follow and grab Angel's dealer, John, had done as they were told. They were instructed to rough the old beach cowboy up a bit, but not to really hurt him.

Eason received a phone call from his men saying they had grabbed him and tossed him in their trunk. When they got to the remote spot they had chosen, the man was dead. They suspected he died of a heart attack while in the trunk. Theorizing the alligators would quickly dispose of the body, they dropped his body in the Shark River. A passing fisherman found John's body before the alligators did. Eason asked Becky Denton, the young, well-connected newspaper reporter, to check her sources. The Sheriff's Department had no leads but were suspicious based on the old beach cowboy's past.

With Angel no longer selling in the Lower Keys, Tom Eason had to fill the vacuum or somebody else would. He asked his group's opinion on how they should handle the lucrative area but only received shaking heads and shrugged shoulders as an answer. All except for the pretty, red-headed reporter, who gave a shy smile and raised her hand just above the table.

"You want to run the Keys?" asked Eason skeptically.

Becky smiled. "Sure! The money is much better than what I make as a reporter, and I'd get to live in the islands. It gets me out of Miami."

Eason's first thought was "No way," but after a few moments, it started to make more and more sense to him. "Hmm," he said. "Let me think that over."

***

The search of the areas defined by the Gulfstream flight, in and around the Able Santamaria airport and other areas towards the coast, including photographing a private airstrip near Isabela, yielded no sightings of the Beaver. The two Cuban operatives assigned to the task ate lunch in Isabela. Had they had asked the bartender about a recent floatplane visit, he likely would have given them all the information they needed to solve the case. They ate their lunch while quietly enjoying the views before driving back to Havana and filing a hollow report.

A few weeks after Orv and Alice arrived at the plantation, Leah returned for a short visit. Her husband had granted her an uncontested "quickie" divorce and resigned his position with Chamberlin Medical in order to avoid a number of civil lawsuits that were threatened by the new board of directors of Chamberlin. Two days after his divorce was final, as Doug Marchbanks was moving into a small apartment in Irvine, he was arrested by the FBI for numerous counts of securities fraud.

The search for DEA Agent Alice Weingarten would take place in the United States, the Bahamas, Cuba, and many other locations throughout the Caribbean. The FBI, the DEA, and numerous other agencies would participate in a search that would turn up nothing concrete. Hundreds of leads would be investigated, thousands of man hours would be expended, but eventually, the investigation into Agent Weingarten's disappearance would become another cold case.

Nearly six months after Alice disappeared, Agent Johnny Reno was sitting in his office, Alice's old office, when a clerk delivered a small packet of mail. On top of the rubber band bound stack was a postcard showing either a sunrise or a sunset. It was such a generic scene that it could have been sold at any gift shop near any beach in the world. He turned it over and saw a simple handwritten note. *"I'm good. A. W."* Johnny immediately noticed that there wasn't a postmark or a stamp on the card. He wondered how it could go through the postal system without either. If it hadn't been mailed normally, how had the card gotten to the building's mailroom? He smiled, then read the words one more time before feeding it into the shredder next to his desk. He never mentioned the postcard to another soul.

In the Keys, after a brief shortage, the flow of marijuana continued across the islands. Those who bought regularly noticed a better grade of weed and even slightly lower prices. One night a week, from ten thousand feet, a regularly scheduled cargo plane flying from the Bahamas to New Orleans would drop two 55-gallon barrels into the strait near Water Key. Tracking devices inside the barrels made them easy to find in the darkness. A body washed ashore in Puerto Rico, identified as Angel Moritz, was found the same day that Becky Denton purchased an expensive condo in Key West. The game of cat and mouse between the smugglers and American authorities continued, always evolving, always changing.

It would be more than a year before Orv's Beaver would emerge from the hangar sporting a fresh coat of paint, a new interior, and a legitimate Cuban registration and tail number. The old drug plane and its crusty pilot would spend their years flying tourists and fishermen to locations around Cuba's Bay Islands.

On a sugar plantation in the Villa Clara Province of Cuba, Orv and Alice's second wedding was attended by the plantation's employees, their families, and a number of local dignitaries. At the reception, the employees of *Valle de Sagua* and the other guests were asked to sit at lavishly appointed tables while the groom helped carve a roasted pig. The bride and groom, along with the plantation's owner, served those in attendance like they were distinguished guests. It was unlike any wedding the Cubans had ever attended.

The Unidentified Man

By Jim Morris

Lightning cracks the western sky
A storm is fast approaching
The surf churns white with rollers
Crashing on the shore
A noise above the rumble
And a seaplane makes a landing
Every night's a big adventure
It's just a job and nothing more

He's had a hundred thousand beers or more
To forget some girl named Alice
And a thousand sleepless nights
Reliving the horrors of the war
A scheme to make a fortune
Got him thrown out of Jamaica
Spent last night with a stranger
Woke up naked on the floor

You might see him for a moment in the darkness where he
stands
A figure hiding, just a shadow leaving footprints in the
sand
A face forgotten, when he disappears
The unidentified man

He's had it with the girls
Who don't meet you at the station
And the partners who befriend you
Then take the goods and run
Dogs who jump their fences

And those whores who can't be trusted
Every tragic ending
Is a story just begun

You might see him for a moment in the darkness where he
stands
A figure hiding, just a shadow leaving footprints in the
sand
A face forgotten, he disappears
The unidentified man

Someday he'll be the body
Washed ashore in Puerto Rico
Or the man found in the wreckage
Of the plane that crashed and burned
In a bar in North Miami
His buddies will toast their fallen comrade
Savoring their whiskey
And just waiting for their turn

He's had a hundred thousand beers or more
To forget some girl named Alice
And a thousand sleepless nights
With the horrors of the war
Survivors of this madness
Live like royalty down on South Beach
Every night's a big adventure
It's just a job and nothing more

ABOUT THE AUTHORS

Jim Morris was an articulate singer/songwriter with a devotion to storytelling.

In the early '90's, Jim quit his corporate career to pursue his music. His fans, once stretching across all of Florida, soon followed him from around the world. As his fan base grew, he spread his wings, playing shows from Belize to Tahiti, around the U.S., Canada, and the Caribbean.

Unfortunately, in July of 2016, while touring with his band in Seattle, Jim died suddenly. His music and his legacy, however, refuse to die, carried on by his band and thousands of rabid fans.

Jim's twenty-seven albums are filled mostly with original music that he wrote while staked out on a beach or floating on his boat. They continue to thrill his fans and inspire the hundreds of musicians who follow in his now well-established path.

Author Dan Sullivan first met Jim and Sharon Morris in Key West in October of 2000. After that fortuitous meeting, Jim played the next sixteen summers in Idaho. During those trips, Jim and Dan spent time together fishing, golfing, and telling stories on bar stools and river banks. From those conversations came the novel, *Tales from The Land of No Mondays*. A year later Dan and Sharon followed with a second book, *The Tales of Tarpon Jim*

The Tales of the Unidentified Man continues the series, the friendship, and the incredible music of the great Jim Morris.

BOOKS BY
DAN SULLIVAN

(Available on Amazon)

Travels with Amy

The Greatest Patriot

Tales from The Land of No Mondays

The Tales of Tarpon Jim

New York to Montana